REALM QUEST

FOREST OF THE
ANCIENTS

WARHAMMER
ADVENTURES
STORIES IN AN AGE OF FANTASY

REALM QUEST

FOREST OF THE
ANCIENTS

TOM HUDDLESTON

WARHAMMER ADVENTURES

First published in Great Britain in 2019 by
Warhammer Publishing,
Willow Road,
Nottingham, NG7 2WS, UK.

10 9 8 7 6 5 4 3 2 1

Produced by Games Workshop in Nottingham.
Cover illustration by Cole Marchetti.
Internal illustrations by Magnus Norén & Cole Marchetti.

A CIP record for this book is available from the British Library.

ISBN 13: 978 1 78496 979 0

See Warhammer Adventures on the internet at

warhammeradventures.com

Find out more about Games Workshop and the worlds of
Warhammer 40,000 and Warhammer Age of Sigmar at

games-workshop.com

Printed and bound by CPI Group (UK) Ltd, Croydon, CR0 4YY

Contents

The Mortal Realms

Each of the Mortal Realms is a world unto itself, steeped in powerful magic. Seemingly infinite in size, there are endless possibilities for discovery and adventure: floating cities and enchanted woodlands, noble beings and dread beasts beyond imagination. But in every corner of the realms, battles rage between the armies of Order and the forces of Chaos. This centuries-long war must be won if the realms are to live in peace and freedom.

PROLOGUE

Seven months ago...

The kitchen was deep in shadows, the
house around them as silent as a crypt.
They rifled through the cupboards as
quietly as they could, Thanis and little
white-haired Marlo, stuffing anything
edible into the cloth sacks they carried.
It was an old place, crumbling and
ramshackle like most buildings in the
city of Lifestone, notable only for a
large painted sign outside: DONZIGER,
it had read, MYSTIC BOTANIST.
TRESPASSERS WILL SUFFER. But
only Marlo could read it and even he
didn't know what half the words meant,
so they'd broken in anyway, finding a

loose window on the ground floor. It was their first stroke of luck, and also their last.

Thanis didn't enjoy thieving, but what choice did she have? The Scraps needed to eat. That was what their little gang called themselves: they were the leftovers of Lifestone, orphans and runaways. They were all young and all poor, but they were a family of sorts and they watched each other's backs.

Still, it was no way to live. The future had been on Thanis's mind a lot lately, the knowledge that she was growing up fast and had no prospects besides stealing. She dreamed of doing something that mattered, bringing good into the world. She'd wanted to join the Lifestone Defenders – she was the right age and she had the muscle – but they wouldn't take a street rat like her. Her fear was that she'd end up in one of the big gangs, the Scarlet Shadow or the Rotten Angels, beating people up for money. She'd rather starve.

She was so lost in thought that she didn't see the stack of plates until she'd already blundered into them. The sound was deafening, a clatter that could surely be heard all through the house. Marlo turned, his eyes wide as moons. Thanis winced apologetically. She wasn't just getting too old for this life, she was getting too big and clumsy too.

A door creaked. For a moment they froze.

Then Thanis sprang into action, shouldering her sack and bolting for the window. She tried to help Marlo up, his hands scrabbling on the sill. But a voice called out, 'Don't move!' and she pulled him down as something thudded into the wall overhead – a throwing axe.

Thanis gulped. The place had looked so run-down, she'd been expecting a couple of house servants at most. But whoever this was, they meant business.

She peered over the counter. Two men stood in the doorway grasping sturdy pikes. They were clad from head to toe in peculiar armour – padded leather gloves, shin-guards and helmets, and breastplates patterned with a four-leafed flower surrounding a mouth filled with thorns.

'Come out,' one called, 'or we'll have to wake our master. Trust me, you don't want that.'

They snickered and Thanis felt a chill. What was this place?

Marlo tugged her sleeve, pointing a trembling finger. 'L-look. Over there.'

In the corner, almost hidden by the shadows, a small trapdoor was set into the floor – some sort of waste disposal, Thanis suspected. She nodded and they scrambled over, the stairs creaking behind them as the guards advanced. Marlo lifted the hatch; below it, all was blackness, a narrow brick-lined tunnel leading straight down. Thanis peered in, wondering if this was really the best idea. Then another axe hit the floor nearby and she shoved Marlo in, the boy tumbling into the dark.

She jumped down after him, the walls closing on all sides. A thought leapt into her mind – what if they narrowed so much that they were trapped, stuck here like rats in a chimney?

Then she crashed through another trapdoor, seeing Marlo's startled face in lamplight as she landed in something warm and sticky. She breathed a sigh, and looked around.

They were in a large metal container, and Thanis stifled a cry as she realised it was filled with wriggling shapes – some sort of larvae, fat and faintly glowing like squishy white ghosts. Lots of them had been flattened as she fell, and they were leaking luminous yellow slime.

She helped Marlo up, then she heaved herself out. 'Why would anyone need all these disgusting grubs?'

'Maybe they're b-breeding insects,' Marlo said, wiping the slime from his face. 'Or they could be feeding something bigger.'

Thanis shuddered. 'We need to get out of here.'

They were in a long corridor with soft purple walls. They could hear the guards' voices coming from up above – they couldn't follow the children through the chute, not in that padded armour, but if they took it off... She picked a direction, tugging Marlo through a swinging door into another corridor with arched entrances on both sides. It curved right and they followed, through a shadowed hall and into yet another corridor. The house was bigger than it had looked from the outside, bigger than it had any right to be.

'I wish Kaspar was here,' Marlo said as they ran. 'He's the best thief in the city. This wouldn't have happened to him.'

'I'm trying my best,' Thanis said. 'Anyway, Kaspar's been gone for days, no one knows where he is.'

Marlo looked up in surprise. 'But I thought he was your best friend?'

'He is,' Thanis said, tight-lipped. 'And I'm sure he's fine. Wherever he's got to.'

They could hear shouts behind them; the guards hadn't given up the chase. They climbed a set of winding steps, losing their bearings entirely. Then Thanis shoved through a final door and skidded to a halt, taking a startled breath. Marlo came up behind her, his mouth dropping open.

The ceiling of the space they'd stumbled into was several storeys high and made of large glass panes, all locked in a steel frame. Through it Thanis could see the distant moon, and beneath that a line of trees – a way out? Where the sloping roof met the ground she could even see a door, standing open.

The problem was that between them and the exit was what could only be described as a jungle – a mass of foliage rising towards the roof, festooned with vines and creepers and huge flowers of a sickly yellow colour that made her eyes hurt. A path ran through the tangle of trunks but she was reluctant to take it; these plants looked... well, she couldn't explain it, but they looked *wrong*.

Thanis had lived in Lifestone all her life, never setting foot outside the city walls. Bricks and stone she knew and trusted; growing things were beyond her comprehension. People who left the city got eaten by dire wolves or lost in swamps, and she had no desire for that to happen to her.

Marlo tugged her hand as shouts rose behind them. 'Come on,' he said. 'It's not far.'

They pushed into the undergrowth, parting the fronds like nervous explorers. There was a rustle, and Thanis's head snapped round. Did something just move? Vines snaked across the path and nodding stems loomed on every side, topped with golden night-blooms bigger than cartwheels. The air was sickly sweet, with a smell like boiled honey and rotting meat.

Then the rustling came again, and this time she saw what made it – one of the vines on the path slithered away as though guarding itself from her blundering feet.

Marlo saw it too and gulped. 'Do you think they're... dangerous?'

Thanis frowned. 'They're plants – they can't hurt us. Right?'

'What about the Sylvaneth?' Marlo asked. 'They're plants and I heard they talk, and walk, and–'

'What is the meaning of this?' a voice boomed, just in front of them. They ducked back, hearts racing. 'What are you doing in here, disturbing my beauties?'

'We discovered thieves in the kitchens, your... masterfulness,' another voice said, and Thanis saw the pair of guards approaching. 'We think they came this way.'

She peered through the fronds. A

man stood by the glass door, wearing a long green robe. His fleshy face was pink with anger as he confronted the guards – they must've taken a different path, she realised, one that didn't lead straight through the jungle. She looked at their padded armour and wondered. It was all starting to make some kind of disturbing sense.

'Thieves?' the man barked, spittle flying from his lips. 'Didn't they see my sign?' Then he smiled. 'Ah, but perhaps this is for the good. My darlings haven't had a good feed for some time, have you? Had to survive on these filthy fleshgrubs.'

He reached into his robe, pulling out a handful of larvae, and tossed them into the undergrowth. The plants twitched hungrily.

Thanis glanced towards the door. Through it she could see an open lawn, and a wall just low enough to vault over. But how to get past without being seen?

There was a shout and one of the

guards spun round. A tendril had snaked from the bushes, brushing his neck. He raised his pike, but the old man held him back. 'They won't strike unless provoked.'

Thanis bit her lip. An idea was forming. A terrible idea, but the only one she had.

Pressing a finger to her lips she led Marlo forwards, trying not to disturb the plants rising around them. Now they were just a short distance from the door, and almost in view of the guards.

'When I say go,' she whispered, 'run as fast as you can.'

Marlo nodded silently. Thanis felt her heart thump. This was either the bravest thing she'd ever done in her life, or the stupidest.

With a roar she leapt to her feet, throwing herself at the nearest guard and shoving him with all her might. He yelled in surprise as he tumbled into the wall of plants, his pike clattering to the floor.

The effect was sudden and startling. Tendrils writhed like furious serpents, wrapping around the guard's arms as he struggled to free himself. He shrieked as more lashed around his ankles, yanking him off his feet. Thanis could never be sure what happened next – she had the impression of a great yellow flower opening like a mouth, ringed with thorns, pulsating horribly. The guard vanished inside; there was a wet gulping sound and a single scream, quickly silenced.

'Go!' she shouted as Marlo scrambled for the door. The second guard was turning, lowering his pike to defend himself. But more creepers spiralled from the undergrowth, suckers latching on to his padded breastplate. The old man raised his hands, crying a string of mystical syllables that jarred on Thanis's ears as she shoved Marlo forwards. She could feel the night air on her face.

They were going to make it.

Then a tendril lashed from the bushes, grasping on to Marlo's exposed arm. He tried to pull away but the vine had taken hold, bulbs of stinging venom bursting on his skin. The tendril tightened and he was tugged off his feet, dragged away from the open doorway.

Thanis grabbed his ankles, pulling in the opposite direction. But the plant was too strong; Marlo howled as his muscles stretched. Thanis cursed. There was only one thing for it.

Dropping Marlo, she bared her teeth, launching herself at the tendril holding him. As she bit down she tasted vile sap and her tongue went numb, but she didn't stop until the vine ripped in two, the severed stump writhing and spurting. Marlo dropped back and Thanis caught him, hoisting him on her shoulder and staggering through the doorway. The wall rose ahead of her and she clambered up, over and away into the dark.

By the time they reached Bowerhome, the sun was coming up. The old mansion didn't belong to the Scraps, of course; its only official occupant was a scatterbrained old woman named Adila, who swore that the Aelf-folk had built the place, and that one day they would return. Thanis couldn't imagine it – the house and gardens were full of shadows and whispers, of tumbling stone and dry waterways, of arched dead trees that might have bloomed once but were now just skeletal outlines.

The other Scraps jumped up as they entered, gathering round. Adila fetched her satchel, pulling out a bronze pot wrapped in muslin. She dipped her fingers in, and smeared a green balm on Marlo's arm.

'Extract of pancia root for the swelling, and a little drop of ulm oil for the pain. I learned this from the Aelves, you know. They were the best healers, so full of wisdom. I recall, one time—'

Thanis cleared her throat. The old woman could ramble for hours if she wasn't interrupted.

Adila blinked, focusing on Marlo's wound. 'Yes, from the Aelves,' she muttered. 'Though someone told me that they might have got it from the Sylvaneth, the tree-people.'

'You saw a Sylvaneth?' Marlo asked excitedly. The mark on his arm was already starting to fade.

Adila sighed. 'No. But I know they

used to visit Lifestone, once in a long while. They're said to still haunt the Forest of the Ancients, out beyond the Everlight River, though that may be rumour.'

Thanis frowned. She'd heard tales of the Sylvaneth – towering treelords, mystical branchwyches and fierce tree-revenants. Some of the kids found them thrilling but she didn't see the appeal – trees that could think, and walk, and kill? That was her worst nightmare.

Her own room was just along the passage, a square chamber with a skylight in the ceiling. She entered and closed the door, ready to drop. Then something moved in the shadows and she froze.

'Show yourself. I've had a long night and I'm not in the mood for games.'

'You mean you're not happy to see me?' a voice asked, a pale face emerging into the light. Kaspar's black hair was a spiky mess, his cloak loose around his skinny body. But his hollow eyes flashed with delight as Thanis strode forwards, grabbing him with both hands and pulling him close.

'Where have you been?' she demanded. 'And what are you doing lurking in the dark?'

Kaspar grinned. 'I like lurking in the dark, you know that.'

'I've been worried,' Thanis said. 'We thought you'd been caught, or hurt, or...'

'I was caught,' Kaspar said. 'Me, the best thief in Lifestone. Embarrassing. But I broke into the Arbour. I know, we always said it was too risky because of that old man, that Shadowcaster. I remember your exact words – *of all the spooky loners in this city, he's the spookiest.*'

'I may have changed my mind,' Thanis said, thinking of the botanist and his carnivorous plants.

'Well, it turns out he's not so spooky anyway,' Kaspar said. 'In fact, he's kind of amazing. I don't know why I broke in, I suppose I felt like a challenge. And I figured there'd be artefacts in there – healers' stuff from the old days. And there were, but he found me before I could steal any of it.

'Actually it was this boy who caught me. His name's Elio, the Shadowcaster's pupil. Nice kid but sort of serious. Anyway, they were discussing what to do with me when the boy saw my birthmark and his eyes went all big, like–'

He demonstrated, and Thanis laughed.

'Vertigan, that's the Shadowcaster's real name, he said he'd been looking for kids with a mark like that. Elio has one, and Vertigan too. He said they're important. When all the marks are brought together something will happen, something that can help the city, and maybe even the whole realm.'

'But I've got a mark like that, too,' Thanis said, exposing her wrist.

'I know,' Kaspar grinned. 'That's what

I told Vertigan, and he wants to meet you.'

Thanis stared into his shadowy grey eyes. Had he been magicked, somehow – had this Vertigan put a spell on him?

'I'm still me,' Kaspar insisted, as though reading her thoughts. 'I promise.'

Thanis reached beneath her blanket, pulling out the tiny pouch she kept there and dropping the coin it contained into her palm. 'Faces I'll come with you and see this Vertigan for myself,' she said. 'Crowns I'm staying here.'

Kaspar smiled. 'Fair enough.'

Thanis balanced the coin on her fingers, willing it to pick the right path. Then she flipped, and watched it spiral up into the air.

CHAPTER ONE

The Burn

Elio lay on the balcony beneath the dome, his brown eyes wide and sightless. Thanis crouched, touching his cheek. His skin was cold. Kiri leaned in, inspecting the purple-veined burn in the centre of the boy's forehead. Alish clutched his hand and Kaspar just looked away, biting his lip.

The mark had been made by a fragment of warpstone, a mystical crystal that the ratlord Kreech had pressed into Elio's head. They'd barely escaped the Skaven, fleeing back to their home at the Arbour, the crumbling palace in the city of Lifestone. At first,

Elio's wound hadn't seemed too serious, just a fading red circle. But then he'd passed out, here on the high platform under the dome of the Atheneum, the great library that lay at the Arbour's heart.

'We should go to his father,' Kiri said, breaking the silence. 'We should ask him for help.'

'I think Lord Elias might be a bit busy,' Kaspar said, gesturing down through the coloured glass. In the valley beyond the city wall spectral

lights blazed, surrounded by legions of shadowy figures. The dark army had come in the night, encircling the city.

'What do they want?' Thanis wondered out loud. 'And why aren't they attacking? Look at those ladders, those siege engines. They could scale the walls any time they wanted. It's not like the Lifestone Defenders could do anything about it.'

'That's exactly why we should find Lord Elias now,' Kiri argued. 'Before things get even worse.'

'But Elio told us not to,' Alish protested, squeezing the boy's hand. 'He said they haven't spoken in ages.'

'This is more important than some family squabble,' Kiri insisted. 'The lord will have money, and he'll know the best healers.'

'But there are no good healers left in Lifestone,' Thanis argued. 'They all went away when... when everything changed.'

None of them knew what had happened to the city in which they lived. In recent decades it had gone from a thriving place of learning and healing to a half-deserted ruin. The only one who might have known was their master Vertigan, but he'd been kidnapped by the Skaven on the orders of a mysterious woman, leaving only his staff behind.

'Thanis is right,' Kaspar said. 'There are some who claim to be medics, but they're just as likely to make him worse. And this isn't some ordinary burn – it's a magical injury.'

'Adila would know what to do,' Thanis told him, remembering the old woman from Bowerhome. But she was gone now, passing away peacefully in her sleep just a few weeks after Thanis and Kaspar left for the Arbour. 'She always said the Aelf-folk were the best healers. Them and the Sylvaneth.'

Kiri looked surprised. 'The walking trees? They're a myth, aren't they?'

'They're real,' Thanis said. 'They're meant to live out beyond the

Stonewoods, past the Everlight River. The place the old folks call the Forest of the Ancients. They even used to come to Lifestone, in the times before.'

'But the Sylvaneth don't help humans,' Kaspar said. 'Remember the story Marlo used to love, about the foolish thief who hid his gold in the forest, and the Sylvaneth turned him into a tree?'

'But they let his son go,' Thanis reminded him. 'The babe, remember? The tree-folk left him outside the city walls. They were kind because he was so little.'

'Elio's not a baby,' Kiri pointed out. 'And the woods are dangerous. I heard men have disappeared out there.'

'So what are we meant to do?' Thanis asked, a strange certainty building inside her. 'Just sit here and watch him suffer? I mean, I hate trees and nature and all of that stuff. The thought of seeing a Sylvaneth scares me to death. But it's Elio's life we're talking about. He saved us in the warren, now it's our turn to help him.'

'And what about the army camped outside our walls?' Kaspar asked. 'Are we meant to fight our way through?'

Thanis cursed. She hadn't thought of that.

'I, um...' Alish said nervously. 'I might have a way we can get out of the city.' And she lowered her gaze down into the old library, where a large black shape hung suspended in the shadows.

'Are you *joking*?' Kaspar asked. 'Please, tell me you're not serious.'

Alish had been working on her flying machine for months, but so far she'd been unable to get it off the ground. It was a huge, unwieldy thing, the patched canvas balloon supporting a wooden gondola festooned with steam-pipes and furnaces.

'I'm this close to making it work,' Alish insisted, holding up her thumb and forefinger. 'Give me one night, and in the morning we'll fly out of here.'

Kiri frowned dubiously. 'You're sure we

wouldn't just crash?'

Alish nodded. 'I'm sure. We can save him, I swear.'

Thanis gritted her teeth. 'I'm in,' she said. 'I trust you, Alish.'

'Me too,' Kiri said. 'But this is a big decision. Not just the airship, but the tree-people, too. Everyone has to agree, or we don't go.'

They looked at Kaspar, who gave a long, uncertain sigh. 'Well,' he said at last. 'I suppose if we all die horribly there'll be no one left to say I told you so.'

They made Elio comfortable on the floor of the Atheneum, covering him with blankets and stacking pillows beneath his head. His skin was ashen and his breathing was shallow, twisted purple vines snaking from the centre of his burn. Kiri volunteered to watch over him while Alish started work on her flying machine, its pipes hissing as she stoked the boiler.

'Watching her won't make it any less terrifying,' Kaspar said, taking Thanis's arm. 'Come on, let's try and get some sleep.'

They wound through the corridors of the Arbour towards their respective sleeping quarters.

'I hope the Scraps are okay,' said Thanis, as they turned into the old armoury. 'I promised to check in this week, then all this happened.'

'They'll cope,' Kaspar said. 'Marlo's turning into quite the leader, I hear the Scarlet Shadow tried to recruit him. He turned them down, of course. He's a sharp one.'

'He learned that from his hero,' Thanis said. 'Don't blush, it's true. He loved how you always kept a level head, even when everything was going crazy. I wish I could say the same. But I'm scared, Kaspar. Vertigan's gone, Elio's sick, and our only plan is to get in some crazy flying thing and look for a race of talking trees who'll almost certainly murder us. I even lost my lucky penny, the one that convinced me to come here in the first place.'

Kaspar leaned forwards, touching her ear. When he drew back there was a coin shining in his palm. 'It must have been hiding back there all along.'

Thanis laughed. 'Where did you really find it?'

'It fell out of your pocket in the warren. I meant to give it back but I forgot.'

'You're always looking out for me, aren't you?' Thanis asked. 'Whatever happens, you're there.'

'Of course,' Kaspar said. 'And I always will be. One of us falls, the other one catches them. Whatever happens, remember that.'

His face had grown suddenly serious, one hand sliding beneath his robe, touching something at his chest. Thanis saw a string around his neck and wondered – when did Kaspar start wearing a pendant? But then he turned away, and the moment passed.

'See you bright and early,' he said, striding off down the passage.

Thanis watched him go. There was no one she trusted more than Kaspar; he'd saved her neck countless times, and she'd saved his. So why did she feel a sudden chill deep inside, as though something terrible was going to happen?

Because something terrible is going to happen, she reasoned. *We're about to be eaten by trees*. Sighing, she entered her room and closed the door.

CHAPTER TWO

A Flock of Ravens

Kiri came at dawn, crouching beside
the giant's breastplate that Thanis slept
in and shaking her gently. She surfaced
slowly from dark dreams of scampering
Skaven and tall, murderous shrubs.

'Alish reckons we're ready to fly,' Kiri
said, looking round the armoury at
the rows of Aelven pikes and Duardin
hammers, silver swords and wooden
longbows, shields painted with a
thousand different sigils. Her weapon of
choice was a catapult, and she was a
superb shot. But she was clad in just a
simple tunic so Thanis got to her feet,
lifted down a coat of looped leather and

handed it to Kiri.

'This should fit you.'

Kiri slipped it over her head. 'It's perfect.'

Thanis's own breastplate was emblazoned with the twin-tailed comet of Sigmar; she strapped it on, along with a pair of giant steel gloves. She flexed her fingers and the metal creaked, but there was no time to oil them now. She grabbed Vertigan's staff and headed for the door.

Then a thought struck her, and she paused. 'Are you going to be the leader now?' she asked Kiri. 'I mean, someone needs to be. Alish is too young and Kaspar's smart but he's reckless, he needs someone to keep him in line. You got us out of the Skaven warren. You and Elio.'

Kiri blushed. 'I only just got here. I shouldn't be telling you all what to do.'

'But Alish looks up to you,' Thanis said. 'And if it makes any difference I'd choose you too, especially for this. You spent a whole year in the wilderness. I've never been outside the city.'

'But you're strong,' Kiri said. 'The toughest of all of us. Maybe you should lead.'

Thanis shook her head quickly. 'I'm okay in a fight, but I really don't like making decisions.'

Kiri laughed. 'How about the two of us agree to do everything we can to keep the others safe?'

Thanis thought about it, then she nodded. 'It's a deal.'

In the Atheneum the airship hung on its moorings, suspended above the cracked stone floor. The gondola was a wooden oval, the shape Thanis imagined a boat to be, with tapered ends and an ashwood railing. On its prow the stuffed head of a gryph-hound snarled fiercely, and inside was a winding network of cogs and gauges and pipes, steam gushing up into the patchwork balloon that hung overhead, attached to the gondola by a complex series of ropes and struts. Alish and Kaspar were helping Elio in – he was awake but weak, grasping at the rickety rope ladder.

'Alish says we're going to the forest,' he told Thanis as she approached. 'Off on a trip.'

'Um, sure,' she said awkwardly. 'Some fresh air, you'll feel good as new.'

'I couldn't tell him the truth,' Alish whispered when he was settled. 'He'd only try and stop us.'

Kiri nodded. 'If it works he'll be cured, then we can tell him. If it doesn't...' She hoisted her leg over the railing, dropping inside. Thanis followed, trying not to touch anything.

'Now, these are the pressure gauges,' Alish said, gesturing to a row of dials attached to small steel tanks. 'They control how high we go, or how low. And this here,' she gestured to a spoked, upright wheel, 'controls the steering paddles, so we can turn.'

'You'll be the one flying it though, right?' Kaspar asked. 'You did build it.'

'Of course,' Alish said. 'I'm just telling you how everything works, in case something happens. Okay, hang on now. I'm going to take her up.'

She strode the length of the gondola, twisting dials and checking gauges as the pipes hissed overhead. It reminded Thanis of someone playing a complicated musical instrument, albeit one that could explode and kill them all if Alish hit the wrong note. The skin of the balloon began to tighten, ropes creaking as they rose into the air. Amazingly, it was working.

Then there was a thunk, and they stopped. Thanis peered up.

'Please don't tell me you forgot about the ceiling.'

Alish laughed. 'Of course not. Here, pull this.'

She handed over a length of rope, smiling encouragingly. Thanis gave a tug and high above them cogs began

41

to whir, machinery grinding deep inside the walls. She saw iron counterweights descending all around the Atheneum, and looking up she saw the dome cracking into segments and folding back like a flower, steel petals opening to the sky. It was a magnificent sight.

'We're flying,' Kiri said as they drifted up, the mooring ropes falling away. 'I don't believe it.'

They rose through the open dome, and Alish grinned. 'Neither do I.'

A shaft of sunlight pierced the clouds as they rose over the Arbour, with the mountains rising peak on stony peak behind them. The city of Lifestone was spread below like parchment, the streets forming complex circular patterns. Thanis had never noticed it before, but the three main streets seemed to mirror the shape of a concentric rune with a line through it – the same one Elio bore, the mark of Ghyran.

They lifted over the Arbour's wall,

those strange, almost manlike stone
figures standing guard over the palace
and the city below. Alish turned the
wheel and they curved around the
peak of a tower, a pair of bright-eyed
goshawks squawking as they passed.
Thanis could see their nests in the
eyrie, hatchlings gazing in wonder as
the strange ship floated by.

Then she looked past the city walls
to the army beyond, and her heart
tightened. They were like a dark
swarm, filling the valley so densely that
not a scrap of open ground could be
seen. Tattered banners flew above siege
engines built of blackwood, and ugly
trebuchets rose on both sides of the
river. But the soldiers themselves were
indistinct, a scuttling mass wreathed in
shadow.

Suddenly Elio gave a shout, ducking
into the gondola. 'My father,' he said,
gesturing. 'I really don't think he'd
approve of me flying.'

Lord Elias stood on the battlements,

the fountain on his armour gleaming in the sun. He shielded his eyes as the strange shape drifted overhead, and Thanis gave a wave. The lord did not respond.

Then they were above the dark army, and Alish took them higher, soaring towards the clouds. Shouts and catcalls sounded in the valley and Thanis saw arrows arcing through the air. But they were too high to be a target; all the dark legions could do was yell and point.

Then Kiri raised a hand, pointing into the distance. 'What's that? A cloud, or...'

'That's no cloud,' Alish said. 'It's moving too fast.'

'And it's cawing,' Kaspar pointed out. Thanis heard it too, a growing clamour of hoarse cries. She could make out shapes in the dark mass – they were birds, she realised, swarming closer.

Then the ravens were upon them, shrieking and flapping as they

dive-bombed the gondola. Their eyes
were black and so were their feathers,
like scraps of pure darkness given
form and a kind of hideous, scratching
life. The sun was blotted out as they
descended, moving in waves around the
airship.

One swept close to Thanis, claws
outstretched, and she struck out with
the staff. The bird let out a strangled
squawk and plummeted. Another
flapped towards Elio, pecking at his
forehead as though drawn to the

violet scar. Thanis heard a twang and the raven squawked, dropping to the floor of the gondola. Kiri reloaded her catapult.

Kaspar knelt over the fallen raven, inspecting it with horrified fascination. 'The mark. On the wings, look.'

Thanis peered closer. He was right. The birds weren't entirely black; their wings were patterned with silver, forming a single runic symbol. Kaspar drew back his sleeve, exposing his own birthmark.

'It's the same,' he said. 'The rune of Shyish.'

'The Realm of Death,' Thanis said softly.

Then there was a thud and the airship juddered, steam-pumps grinding. They were losing altitude, drifting down towards the waiting army. She saw faces peering up, red eyes glaring hungrily. Some of the soldiers were very pale and thin, and they waved swords in their sticklike arms.

Alish reached for the controls. 'One of those birds must have got in the works. I can fix it, I just—'

More ravens swooped in suddenly, angling towards Alish as though they knew what she was trying to do. They pecked and clawed, tangling in her hair, wings flapping at her face. Thanis sprang forwards, grabbing a raven in each of her gloved fists and yanking them away, strands of Alish's hair still clutched in their vicious, swiping claws. The birds writhed and screeched but Thanis held them firmly, flinging them over the side of the airship.

Kiri joined her and they formed a defensive wall around Alish as she checked the gauges, banging on the pipes with the flat of her hand, trying to shift the blockage. More of the birds plunged in but Kiri aimed her catapult, taking two of them down in quick succession. Thanis hefted Vertigan's staff, and felt three satisfying collisions as she swung it around, and another two as she brought it back down. Kaspar had grabbed one of the mooring ropes and was swinging it like a whip, striking ravens left and right.

Then Alish gave a victorious shout and the steam-pumps caught, vapour gushing up into the balloon. They rose once more and the ravens peeled away, retreating in a tattered flock.

'That's right!' Alish said, shaking a fist. 'Don't you mess with the crew of the...' She let out a cry, slapping herself on the forehead. 'I forgot! Before we took off I wanted to give this old thing a name. Do you think it's bad luck to do it once you're already in the air?'

'Of course not,' Kiri said. 'How about the *Flying Junkpile*?'

'I prefer the *Deathtrap*,' Kaspar said. 'Or – I know, the *Please Don't Crash and Kill Us All*.'

Alish glowered at him.

'We should call it something that reminds us of where we came from,'

Thanis said. 'How about the *Pride of Lifestone*?'

'That's a bit serious,' Alish said. 'What about the *Arbour Seed*? It does look a bit like a seed pod, after all.'

'*Arbour Seed*,' Kiri nodded. 'I like it.'

'Me too,' Thanis smiled. 'Elio, how about you? Any more suggestions?'

But he was slumped on the floor, his eyes shut.

He must have lost consciousness during the attack, Thanis thought, *but we were all too busy to notice.*

They knelt at his side, making him as comfortable as they could. The mood turned grim once more, as the *Arbour Seed* rose until they were almost touching the clouds. The city had dropped away behind them, the army dwindling too. Below them, all Thanis could see was an ocean of trees, stretching to the far horizon. Most were as big as buildings, their roots and branches coiled around one another. Between them she could see glimmers of light, swarms of sparks flitting among the shadowed trunks. And there were other kinds of movement too – large shapes pushing through the undergrowth, the branches rustling as they went.

'Look,' Alish said softly. 'That must be the Everlight.'

The river wound through the green land, a twisting grey ribbon. It was poorly named, Thanis thought – there was no light in that dark, grim water. She bit her lip as they sailed closer, wondering what in Sigmar's name they thought they were doing.

CHAPTER THREE

Strongstem and Litheroot

Kiri peered into the sky. 'It's past midday, we should think about setting down.'

Alish frowned. 'The thing about that is... well, I've been so busy trying to get this thing to go up, I didn't really think very much about how to get it down again.'

'It's not like there are lots of places to land, anyway,' Thanis said. 'It's just trees everywhere.'

'What about there?' Kaspar suggested, pointing to a patch of exposed, stony ground between the trunks of two huge blackwood oaks.

Alish looked dubious, but she nodded.
'I can give it a try. But you should all hang on.'

She grasped the wheel, steering the *Arbour Seed* around a pair of jutting moss-pines. Then she twisted a dial and they descended, brushing the tops of the trees.

'Considering it's your first time, you're pretty good at this,' Kiri said.

Alish blushed. 'Well I built her, so I know how everything works. I j–'

There was a bone-shaking crunch as the gondola smacked into a heavy branch, almost tipping them out. The balloon let out a hiss, and looking up Thanis saw a puncture in the side, with steam pouring from it. They dropped suddenly, ropes tangling in the bare branches. The gondola hit the ground, steam billowed around them, and Alish twisted the cogs frantically until it subsided.

'You were saying?' Kaspar asked drily as they caught their breath.

Alish shrugged sheepishly. 'We're down, aren't we?'

Thanis looked around. The trees loomed on every side, blocking the light from the watery sun. 'Please tell me we'll be able to take off again. I really don't want to be stuck here.'

Alish looked at the twisted balloon. 'We'll have to patch that hole and someone might have to climb up and cut a few of those branches back, but–'

There was a low rumble and the tree shook, as though in a strong wind.

'I think it heard us,' a voice whispered, and they turned.

Elio was sitting up, rubbing his eyes. His hair was matted with sweat and his burn glowed an angry reddish purple, but his eyes were clear as he looked around.

'Where are we? I remember something about a trip, and my father... but it's all so hazy.'

Thanis helped him to his feet. 'Don't get mad, but we're in the forest. We've come to ask the Sylvaneth to heal you.'

Elio's mouth dropped. 'But they're dangerous! Don't you know the story of the foolish thief?'

'That's what I said,' Kaspar put in. 'They didn't listen.'

'We didn't have a choice,' Thanis argued. 'You're getting sicker. We didn't know what else to do.'

Kiri climbed cautiously out of the gondola, dry leaves crunching beneath her boots. 'So how do we find these... tree-people?'

Kaspar helped Elio down behind her. 'You don't find the Sylvaneth,' he said. 'They find you.'

Suddenly Elio gave a shout and Thanis turned, expecting to see him clutching the burn on his forehead. But instead he was staring down at his birthmark, more surprised than hurt. He touched it gingerly.

'The moment I touched the ground it started to tingle. Does anyone else feel anything?'

They all shook their heads.

Elio faced the wall of trees. 'Look, I know this is crazy but I think it wants me to go that way.'

Kaspar squinted at him. 'Are you sure that burn hasn't muddled up your mind?'

But Kiri shook her head. 'The same thing happened to me in the slave camp, I felt this... I don't know, this calling. It was like my mark was speaking to me, except I couldn't hear it, only feel it. But it led me to

Ghyran, and eventually to Lifestone. If Elio's mark says we go that way, I say we trust it.'

The trees were densely packed, interspersed with thorny thickets and patches of briar. But there was a way between them – not quite a path, more of a natural opening. Elio and Kiri stepped inside, and Thanis was about to follow when Kaspar took her arm.

'Are you sure about this?' he hissed. 'Following a birthmark? It's crazy, isn't it?'

She nodded slowly. 'I guess so. But Kiri seems sure. And we've used them to find each other, haven't we? I don't know, it feels... right, somehow. Come on, I'll protect you.'

At first the going was fairly easy, the five of them moving through pools of shifting shadow and milky light. But soon the trees began to close in, their knotted branches interlocking overhead like a grey-green roof. The ground was sometimes rocky and uneven, at other times soft and squelchy with patches of moss that sucked at their feet. One time Thanis's boot sank so deep that she had to use both hands to pull it free, and as she was doing so she felt something moving, like fingers brushing against her ankle. She tugged her boot out and hurried on.

There were sounds in the forest, too – deep creaks and moans that were neither plant nor animal, but something in between. Chattering swarms of bright fireflies seemed to form shapes as they spiralled in the sunlight – faces, creatures, towers. Vines clung to the trunks of trees like exposed veins, blood-dark blooms bursting open as they passed, letting out a soft sigh.

They stopped in a little glade, waiting while Elio got his breath back. The clearing was dappled in sunlight and ringed with towering yellow-green fronds, the mulchy ground shrouded in a layer of clinging fog. *That's odd*, Thanis thought. There was no mist elsewhere in the forest, only here.

'It's getting late,' Kaspar said. 'I think we should go back.'

Kiri frowned. 'But what about the Sylvaneth? We have to find them or this whole thing's been a waste of time.'

'He's right, if night comes we should be in the *Arbour Seed*,' Thanis said. 'We can defend ourselves there, if anything tries to... you know.'

'Elio, what about you?' Alish asked. 'Do you feel any–'

With a sigh Elio dropped to the ground, like a puppet whose strings had been cut. He landed on his back in a carpet of gold, disturbing the mist around him. His eyes were blank and the burn on his forehead was bright red.

'Hey,' Kiri said, kneeling and touching his face. 'Elio, can you–'

The ground shook suddenly, almost throwing Thanis off her feet. She steadied herself, looking fearfully around the clearing. The slender plants encircling them seemed to weave and sway in an almost hypnotic dance. There was a series of pops and clouds of yellow dust exploded into the air, clouding Thanis's vision. She began to sneeze uncontrollably, her eyes streaming.

Then Alish gave a scream. 'He's moving! Look, it's got him!'

She was right – Elio was sliding unconsciously over the soft ground, dragged by a yellow frond locked fast around his ankle. There was a horrible wet slurping sound and a series of mouth-like holes opened in the damp ground, ringed with bulbous petals. This whole clearing was one giant plant, Thanis realised, a massive growth trying to suck them all in. Kiri loaded her catapult but there was nothing to aim at – just vines and tendrils and a fog of stinging pollen. Tendrils lashed towards Thanis and she swung the staff, crying out in horror.

'Get back, you horrid–'

'ENOUGH!'

The voice was deafening; the ground shook with the force of it, and the snaking vines stopped abruptly. A shadow moved beyond the clearing, but Thanis couldn't make it out.

'Wh-who's there?' she asked. 'Who are you?'

'Who am I?' the voice boomed. 'Who are *you*?' It seemed to emanate from all around them, dry and rough like scraping roots and falling timber.

Kiri took a step. 'We come from Lifestone. We seek the Sylvaneth. We need their help.'

The disembodied voice snorted, whether with anger or amusement Thanis couldn't guess. 'You seek the Sylvaneth? You have found them. But we do not give aid to lost creatures.'

'We're not lost,' Thanis said, standing over Elio. 'Our friend is sick, we were told you could heal h–'

'NO!' the voice thundered furiously.

'We are the guardians of the forest, we do not tend to weak and foolish mortals.'

Alish started to protest but a mass of vines came snaking suddenly from the mist and latched on to her wrists and ankles, pulling her down towards those hideous sucking mouths. They grabbed Kaspar too, yanking him off his feet. He yelled for Thanis, kicking and fighting.

'Let go of my friends!' Thanis cried, swinging the staff and swiping blindly at the vines as they coiled towards her. One had hold of her foot, trying to tug her down. Instinctively she reached for Kiri, gripping the girl's wrist. Kiri stumbled, grabbing at Thanis, and in that moment something happened.

Kiri's eyes went wide with surprise. 'Do you feel that?'

Thanis nodded. There was a strange sensation growing inside her – a kind of confidence, travelling inwards from her wrist to her heart. Looking down she saw that Kiri's hand was tight around her birthmark, and that her own hand was locked around Kiri's. Thanis grinned as the feeling increased, setting her nerves alight.

Then Kiri broke free, swung her catapult around and let loose. One of the vines holding Alish snapped in two, spewing green sap. Thanis drove the staff into the ground, piercing the soft surface of the plant. The living structure shook and groaned, those awful mouths opening and closing as though in pain. The vines let go of Alish and Kaspar and finally Elio, snaking away into the mist.

Kiri lifted the boy to his feet. His head was lolling, his mouth slack. Thanis helped her carry him across the clearing, back into the thick of the forest. She could still feel that strange energy inside her; it wasn't a new strength, she realised – it had been there all along. It was as though a door had been opened when she and

Kiri linked arms, allowing the power to come through.

Then Alish gasped, staring up into the branches. Something stood blocking their way, something vast and dark and motionless. There were eyes in it, huge and silver-green, watching them.

Kaspar took a step back, his hand on his chest. Kiri reached for Thanis and she saw her own feelings reflected in her friend's face – fear, amazement and wide-eyed wonder. The figure before them was sheathed in dry bark like a bronzewood tree, with a crown of tangled thorns and huge, rootlike feet. But most trees didn't have long, outstretched arms, and they certainly didn't speak.

'We took you for Duardin,' the Sylvaneth said. 'When we first saw your flying machine. But now we see you are human children. Tell me, how did you free yourselves from the dragonflower?'

Thanis and Kiri let Elio down as gently as they could, and placed their hands on their weapons.

'They're afraid, Strongstem,' said another voice, softer and more musical, like raindrops on a hollow log. 'You have terrified them.'

A second Sylvaneth emerged from the brush – this one was shorter and more slender, with shoot-green limbs and eyes the colour of gillyflowers. Her voice and form were somehow feminine, and in the shadows behind her Thanis thought she saw other shapes, small and green like saplings. Sylvaneth children?

Was such a thing possible?

The newcomer pointed to the black symbol on Kiri's wrist. 'It was these marks that gave them the strength,' she said. 'Realm runes, Strongstem. These are no ordinary children.' She turned to them. 'How did you come by these marks?'

'W-we were born with them,' Kiri said.

'We're not completely sure what they mean,' Thanis added. 'Our master, his name was V–'

Kaspar squeezed her arm, shaking his head. 'We shouldn't trust them,' he whispered. 'We don't know what they want.'

Alish stepped forward, gesturing to Elio who lay slumped on the mossy floor. 'Look, our friend is sick. He was wounded with warpstone. Can you help him?'

The first Sylvaneth gave a grunt. 'I told you, we do not heal humans. Plants, yes, and growing things. But not chopping, burning mortals.'

'We haven't burned anything,' Alish protested. 'Elio loves plants, and trees, and all that stuff. He's a good boy, you can't just let him die.'

The slender Sylvaneth knelt, her stemlike fingers brushing the wound on Elio's forehead. He stirred, whimpering, and the Sylvaneth's eyes narrowed. She glanced back at her companion and somehow Thanis knew they were communicating, speaking without words.

Suddenly the Sylvaneth laid her hands on the earth, opening her fingers wide. Green shoots snaked from their tips, twisting towards Elio, wrapping gently around him. Thanis started forwards but the Sylvaneth shook her head.

'Do not be afraid. I will not harm him.'

The roots tucked in close around the boy, and as the Sylvaneth stood he was lifted from the floor, cocooned in a green cradle.

'My name is Litheroot,' she said, placing him across her shoulder. 'I am what we call a branchwych, familiar with the ways of both natural and unnatural magic. The wound your friend bears is... most unusual. It has a power that is known to us.' She beckoned to them. 'My treelord Strongstem has agreed that you may follow us. There is a glade nearby where we can rest and talk.'

'So you'll help him?' Kiri asked.

The treelord turned away. 'If you agree to do as we ask, we shall consider it. For now, just be content to follow.' He moved off, his footsteps shaking the ground.

'Um, sorry, Mr... um, Strongstem,' Alish called out. 'What about my airship? What if something tries to eat it?'

The treelord did not turn around. 'It will be safe. Not a leaf moves in this forest without my permission.'

As he strode away, Thanis looked sideways at Kiri. She could feel eyes in the branches, the whole forest seeming to close in watchfully.

'Do you ever get the feeling you're making a really big mistake?' she whispered.

Kiri pocketed her catapult. 'I know, but what choice have we got?' she asked. 'We're here for Elio.' And she stepped forwards, pushing into the wall of trees.

CHAPTER FOUR

The Elmheart Glade

The sun was low to the horizon now, and the evening shadows were lengthening around them. Even these seemed strange to Thanis, coiling and shifting as though with a mind of their own, making phantom shapes between the branches. Strongstem set a fast pace, stepping easily over hunched boulders and yawning chasms that the children had to clamber over or find a way around. Thanis had noticed that there was a cloud of insects buzzing around the treelord, darting between the boughs and outgrowths that sprouted from his arms and his head.

They seemed to be communicating with one another, screeching and chattering in a language she'd never heard.

She felt something on her bare arm and peered down. One of the creatures crouched on her elbow, silver wings fluttering hypnotically. It wasn't an insect at all but something far stranger, its many-faceted eyes bright in a grinning, weirdly human face. She watched it, fascinated.

Then suddenly the creature lowered its head, exposing a row of thorny fangs and sinking them into her skin. Thanis cried out in pain and surprise, swiping the creature away. It took to the air, yammering irritably.

'We call them spites,' the branchwych explained, striding alongside. 'They mean no harm.'

'It bit me,' Thanis protested, rubbing her elbow.

'You are strange to them,' Litheroot said. 'Perhaps it simply wanted to know what you are made of.'

Thanis put her head down and kept walking. As if the talking trees and giant killer flowers weren't enough, now she had nasty little biting things to contend with. She'd suspected all along that there was nothing outside the city walls worth knowing about, and now she was sure of it.

The light faded and the moon rose, and now the forest became truly unsettling, a trackless labyrinth of shifting shadows and shimmering, far-off lights. Strongstem was just a dark shape among deeper shades – the only way they could follow him was by the sound of his footfalls.

'When will we sleep?' Kiri asked. 'We can't keep going forever.'

'Sylvaneth do not sleep,' Strongstem said, without slowing.

'That's not an answer,' Kiri pointed out.

But it wasn't long before Thanis felt a change in the air, a sweeter scent on the breeze and a warm glow between the branches. Strongstem bowed beneath a canopy of low-hanging trees then he straightened, holding out his arms.

'Behold,' he said. 'The Elmheart Glade.'

Thanis stepped in beside him, and her breath stopped. The glade was vast, larger than the Atheneum, the trees like spires craning inwards, the tips of their massive branches touching high above. Below was a carpet of silver grass, and everywhere she looked she saw Sylvaneth – slender tree-revenants with their bladed scythes, and horn-crested dryads with countless tangled limbs, all surrounded by clouds of chattering spites and showers of shimmering fire-moths.

But all of them were dwarfed by the figure in the centre of the glade, so tall that its highest branches were twined into the roof. At first Thanis thought it was another Sylvaneth, massive but motionless. Then she realised it was a statue formed from living wood, a lattice of trees and shrubs and slender sproutlings all shaped to resemble a woman. The trunks of her legs were knotted with roots, her outstretched arms were wreathed with vines, and her mouth burst with flowers like a song of colour. She wielded an outgrowing blade of mahogany, blacker than the deepest forest shadows.

'Alarielle,' Alish whispered, gazing in wonder.

'The Everqueen,' Litheroot acknowledged, her eyes sparkling. 'She of the Sylvaneth. We come from all across the realm to pay tribute to the

Elmheart statue. There was a battle here once, long ago, though I am too green to recall it.'

'I am not,' Strongstem said, rumbling with centuries-old anger. 'The poison-bringers came with fire and disease to blight the trees and the very soil in which they grew. With Alarielle's blessing we drove them back, though the victory came at great cost. The statue marks the place where their final doom came.' His voice was weary with sorrow for all those who had fallen, and it gave Thanis a sense of how long the Sylvaneth had endured here, how many years they had fought against the darkness that still threatened Ghyran. The great war that she was only just beginning to perceive.

'I must bear your friend away,' Litheroot said, cradling Elio as he lay unconscious. 'And you should all rest. You will have a long day tomorrow.'

The treelord rumbled in agreement. 'A long day indeed,' he said, gesturing to a quiet corner of the glade beneath the shade of a low-growing laurelwort bush. 'Before your friend can be healed, you must fulfil your obligation.'

They looked at one another, and Thanis could see the others fighting back their doubts. She turned to Strongstem and nodded firmly. 'We'll do whatever you want. Just please, help him.'

The morning seemed to come swiftly, pale shafts of sunlight slanting into the glade. Thanis awoke with a cry, feeling a sharp nip on the back of her neck. She swiped roughly and the spite took to the air, buzzing and chittering. Thanis snarled at it.

'That's what you get for trying to bite someone,' she said, and the creature let out a string of what sounded like curses. Then a shadow fell, and she looked up.

Strongstem stood over them, his rooted feet planted in the grass. 'Drink this,' he said, placing a sloshing pail before them. 'Then rise. We have a long way to go.'

Thanis felt stiff and cold, her thoughts clouded and worrisome. They were so far from home, at the mercy of beings whose thoughts and actions were utterly unlike anything she was accustomed to.

Kiri knelt by the pail, cupping her hands and drinking. 'It's good.'

Thanis reached in; the water was ice-cold, but the taste was sweet. As she drank she could feel strength returning to her tired limbs.

'Good,' Strongstem said as the others drank. 'Now, leave nothing behind. You will not return here.'

'But what about Elio?' Alish asked. 'Can't we say goodbye?'

'He is with the healers,' Strongstem said. 'He will be far safer than you will be, out in the wild.'

Thanis felt a shiver, but she gritted her teeth and set off after the treelord, taking Alish's hand. 'Don't be scared,' she said. 'We'll see Elio again, I'm sure of it.'

Alish forced a smile. 'I think so too. These Sylvaneth may talk tough, but deep down I think they're on our side.'

Again Strongstem set a punishing pace, following paths only the Sylvaneth knew. The sun shimmered through the branches, life seeming to spring up everywhere the light touched. Purple flowers unfurled from man-high thickets of thorn, puffing out clouds of sharp-smelling pollen. Patches of flaking fungus spread across towering walls of rock, advancing like a hungry green tide. Mushrooms sprouted from patches of boggy marshland, their caps sparkling like blue crystal. And all around them Thanis heard movement – the swarm of spites and the croak of bullfrogs, and flocks of birds in the high branches, their chatter like mocking laughter. Elio would've been able to name them all, she knew, but to her it was just strange and unnerving.

Sometime in the late morning Strongstem's stride slowed and he gestured to a dark green grove of bushes in the shade of a stony outcropping. The branches were weighed down with gleaming black fruits, and Thanis stepped closer to pluck one.

'These are coal-apples,' the Sylvaneth said. 'Your own people planted them, long ago. Look.'

Following his outstretched limb Thanis saw that the rocky cliff they were resting against was actually the side of a building, a Sigmarite temple half-buried in the foliage. Walls and cracked roofs loomed up ahead, dark with moss and strung with shifting creepers. She saw the tip of a tower above the trees, topped with a creaking weathervane in the shape of Ghal Maraz, the hammer of Sigmar.

'What was this place?' she asked, taking a bite of the apple, the sour-sweet flavour fizzing on her tongue. 'It feels sort of familiar, but that's not possible.'

'This was the city of Everlight,' Strongstem said. 'Named for the river that lies across that ridge.' He pointed to a dark rise with clouds gathered at its peak.

'So where did everyone go?' Alish asked.

Strongstem sighed. 'They were destroyed by the same power that once poisoned the forest. Many of them fought with us to drive back the rot, but they were not as strong as we are. They perished, and these ruins are all that remains.'

'Is... is this what's happening in Lifestone?' Kiri asked in a whisper.

Yes, Thanis thought. That was why the dead city felt so familiar. It had the same sense of fading grandeur as her home.

'I do not know,' Strongstem admitted. 'Such things are not my concern. All I can say is the last time I visited your city it was a place of life and growth, a garden almost fit for Sylvaneth. It would be a shame if Lifestone were to die.'

The afternoon was even more arduous than the morning had been, spent scaling walls of rock and brakes of choking trees. Once they were forced to shuffle along a fallen trunk above a rocky ravine, a whirlpool of milky white water churning in the depths below. A coal-apple fell from Thanis's pocket and she saw it spiralling in the current, sucked away into the fathomless dark. The spites clouded around, biting and mocking, until Strongstem made a deep noise in his throat and the little creatures swarmed away.

On the far side the ground began to ascend, rising towards the ridge. But as they climbed Strongstem's pace seemed to slow, his limbs creaking like branches in the wind. Thanis heard a grunt of effort as he stepped over a tumble of boulders, before descending carefully on the far side. She was about to ask him what was happening when she heard a gasp.

Kiri had frozen in her tracks, looking up to where the trees broke at the top of the ridge. Three figures stood motionless, gazing out into the valley beyond. They were Sylvaneth, their arms upraised, their feet rooted. But as Thanis circled around them she saw that their eyes were closed, patches of moss and greyish mould growing on their mouths and outstretched fingers.

'What happened to them?' she asked, touching the dead bark.

'They are... were Sylvaneth,' Strongstem said, his voice somehow robbed of its strength. 'They are the reason I have brought you here.'

He straightened painfully, like an old man with aching joints. Then he pointed down into the valley below. A dark ribbon ran through it, between steep, forested hills.

'That is the Everlight River, the jewel of this forest. It runs east, down to an ancient lake called Rawdeep Mere. The lake is... strange somehow. It always was. Not a haunt of evil, but a place of shadows and visions. But in recent times something has changed. The lake has become... sick.

'We do not know what or who is responsible, because we cannot get close enough to find out. Even here I can feel a power working inside me, sapping my strength, confusing my thoughts...' He broke off, touching his forehead with one huge hand. 'These three are the last Sylvaneth who tried to go any closer. But we do not know what they discovered, because before they could return their life was taken, the power solidifying them from the inside.'

'But you think it won't affect us,' Kiri realised. 'You think we could find out what's happening.'

Strongstem nodded. 'You are not as susceptible to mystical energy. You may be able to discover what is poisoning the mere, and return to tell us.'

Thanis gave a gulp. 'How sure are you that it won't affect us? I mean, I feel all right now, but...'

'It is a risk you must take,' Strongstem told her. 'For the sake of your friend. You see, there is one more thing. The power that has infected Rawdeep Mere has the same sense, the same *smell* almost, as the sickness that has attacked your Elio. We do not know how this is possible, but you may find answers at the lake. Answers that may lead you to... whatever it is that you seek.'

Thanis looked up at Strongstem, wondering if the Sylvaneth knew more than he was letting on. But before she could speak she heard a desperate whining and buzzing, and saw the cloud of spites around his head whirling madly.

The treelord raised his mighty fists. 'Shelter behind me, all of you.

Something is coming. Quickly!'

The wall of trees exploded as a huge shape emerged onto the ridge, flapping towards them on darkly feathered wings. It was somehow both bird and beast, rearing up on muscled hind legs and lunging at Strongstem with clawed forearms. The Sylvaneth took a step back, raising his arms.

CHAPTER FIVE

Rawdeep Mere

'A griffon,' Strongstem said, facing
the creature. 'But look, it has been
corrupted too.'

The griffon gave a cry and Thanis
saw that it had two hideous heads,
each one tipped with a hooked beak
smeared with dry blood. Its eyes were
black, but in their depths she saw a
purple gleam – the same colour as
Elio's mark.

It sprang and the treelord stepped
back again. His clenched fists were the
size and weight of boulders, but his
movements were slow and the creature's
claws sunk in, cutting three deep

grooves in his exposed forearm. Sap leaked out, running in rivulets to the ground. He took another swing but the griffon darted aside, slicing down with its beak, worrying the green shoots around Strongstem's torso. He gave a grunt of dismay, and retreated another pace.

Then he raised his mighty hands, muttering under his breath. Hearing a dry scrape, Thanis looked down. The ground was alive with shifting roots, breaking from the soil and snaking towards the unsuspecting griffon. One of them lashed around its shaggy tail, dragging it backwards. The two heads screeched as the beast kicked furiously, struggling and howling.

Then its left-side head darted and the roots flew free, sliced in two by that razor-sharp beak. It kicked and more of the vines snapped, the great beast fighting free. Strongstem shook his massive head, trying to summon his strength.

'He's weak,' Kaspar said. 'This... power must be getting to him.'

Thanis gulped. If the treelord lost, the griffon would gulp them down without stopping for breath. 'He was stronger back there,' she said, gesturing down the slope. 'We need to draw it away.'

She took a step forwards, slamming the staff onto a flat stone. The knock rang out in the still air.

'Hey!' she shouted. 'Over here!'

The griffon turned, lowering its heads. Thanis knocked again and Kiri waved her arms. Kaspar and Alish began to retreat, back towards the line of trees.

Then the creature sprang, bounding towards them. Thanis broke, Kiri on her heels. They sprinted for the treeline, the monster right behind them. Thanis felt its hot breath on her neck as they scrambled down the slope. She swiped back with the staff and felt it make contact. The griffon shrieked as the trees closed in.

Then she heard a shout and saw

Kaspar standing frozen, his eyes wide. Alish stopped too, and Thanis turned, skidding in the dirt, using the staff to keep herself upright.

The griffon was still lunging at them, its beak snapping. But it was no longer advancing – it was held in place, claws scrabbling at the ground. Raising her head Thanis saw Strongstem standing firm, his feet planted in the earth and his massive fist wrapped around the creature's tail.

The beast turned, snapping furiously. Strongstem opened his hand and the griffon sprang free.

The treelord drew himself up, working his shoulders, loosening his stiffened limbs. Then he drove his fists together once, twice, with a sound like falling boulders. The griffon accepted his challenge, springing forward with its beaks raised for the attack.

But Strongstem's fists swept in from both sides at once, pinning the creature between them. Thanis saw its eyes bulge as its twin heads slammed together. The griffon reeled, wings flapping as it tried to retreat. Strongstem swung again, upwards this time, knocking the creature off its feet and into the air.

The griffon twisted, beating its wings desperately. It gave a shriek of rage then it lifted, flapping raggedly into the darkening sky. They saw it rise above the ridge, struggling to clear the tops of the trees. It gave a last squawk of pain and fury, then it was gone.

Strongstem sank back, sitting so hard that the ground shook.

'Thank you,' he said. 'I could not have fought it alone.' He stared after the griffon, his eyes brimming with anger. 'That was a noble beast, once. A hunter of the high passes. How did it come to be here, so far from home? The dark power must have lured it somehow, twisting it out of shape. It is spreading.'

He looked at them, his eyes reflecting

the last light of the sinking sun.

'Go,' he said. 'Follow the river. Find out who did this so we can tear them apart.'

Kiri shouldered her pack and Alish tightened her tool belt. Kaspar raised his hood, and Thanis reached out to touch Strongstem on the arm.

'We won't let you down,' she promised.

The way down to the valley floor was part climb, part scramble, the children clinging to rocks and roots as they descended towards the Everlight River. The sky was fading as they broke out onto the bank, the rush of water loud in their ears. Thanis looked back to the dark ridge where Strongstem waited. But they were on their own now; if they got into trouble, he wouldn't be able to help them.

They followed the river downstream, clambering over boulders and through patches of muddy mire, shinning down the sheer sides of shallow waterfalls

and skirting silent pools. The water was
black beneath the darkening sky, but as
the moon rose a change came over the
river – in its depths were little sparks
of light, circling as they were swept on
the current. And as night deepened the
river came alive, glowing with dancing
shards of blueish white, like fragments
of trapped moonbeam.

'Are those things... alive?' Thanis
asked, peering into the gleaming water.

A shape rose to the surface, opening
its mouth to swallow a swirling speck.
The fish's face glowed for a moment,
beams shining from its open eyes. Then
it swallowed, and the light was gone.

After a while the river opened out,
rolling between banks of sedge-grass
and rustling broomweed. Kiri strode on
ahead, eager to find the lake and get
this done. Alish hung close to Thanis,
convinced that the griffon was about to
reappear, or some other creature just
as hideous. Kaspar brought up the rear,
and when Thanis glanced back she saw

his hand inside his robe again, touching the pendant around his neck. Suddenly she thought of the pyramid Kiri had given him, a gift from some mysterious apothecary she'd met in Lifestone, a woman who claimed to be Kaspar's mother. Could that be it?

Then Kiri gave a shout, squinting in the hazy light. There was a mound of earth on the riverbank and she began to climb, beckoning as she reached the top. 'Quick, look at this. It's... horrible.'

Thanis clambered up, Alish close behind her. The mound was just the start of it – up ahead was a series of huge wooden structures, like walls planted in the earth. Only they weren't walls, Thanis saw; they were a dam, built to block the course of the Everlight River and divert it into a great channel leading south into the forest.

'Someone's moved the river,' Kaspar said in amazement. 'Why would they...'

'To do that,' Kiri said. 'Look.'

Ahead was the old riverbed, a dry
conduit lined with stones and gravel.
And beyond that was a great hole in
the earth, a deep crater of sloping
mud and rocky inclines, so huge and
deep that Thanis couldn't even see the
bottom, let alone the other side.

'Rawdeep Mere,' Alish said. 'They've
drained the whole lake. But why?'

'I don't know,' Kiri said. 'But I know
where to look for answers.'

In the distance was a faint purple
glow, the same colour as the mark on
Elio's forehead and the light in the
griffon's eyes. It shone in the bed of
the lake, pulsating silently.

'Come on,' Thanis said. 'Let's get
closer.'

They clambered down to the dry
riverbed. The huge earthworks loomed
over them, the wooden walls held up by
stanchions sunk into the ground. The
water inside was deafening, rushing
and roaring as it was diverted from
its natural course into that wide,

purpose-built channel. The empty lake stretched ahead of them, patches of mud and rotten weeds interspersed with narrow expanses of stony ground. They followed one of these, hurrying towards the purple gleam in the distance.

There were shapes half-sunk into the mud, the rotting carcasses of water-going beasts, their exposed bones gleaming in the moonlight. The smell was hideous. A shadow blocked the moon and Thanis looked up to see a black hulk standing over them – the side of a ship, gleaming with barnacles and black weeds. There was a hole in the stern and she realised the craft must have been sunk here centuries before, perhaps during the same conflict that had wiped out the population of Everlight.

There were forms scattered in the mud around the ship's prow, objects of white and bronze. Drawing closer she saw empty eye sockets and jutting ribs, skulls encased in battered helmets and

skeletal hands clutching rusty swords. They had drowned or died in battle, their bones lain on the bottom of the mere. She wondered if they were noble or cruel, fighting to protect the realm or destroy it. It didn't much matter: they were dead either way.

The glow on the horizon was brighter now, shafts of purple light filling the air. They crunched across the lakebed on a floor of loose stone, keeping their heads low and trying to stay quiet. Another shape rose over them – some kind of blubbery freshwater leviathan, its black eyes turned to the moonlit sky, its pointed carapace ringed with clusters of bright red tentacles. Was it her imagination, Thanis wondered, or did she see one of them move?

A sound was beginning to build ahead of them, a deep, regular thump that shook the ground. They picked up the pace, crossing the shingle to a cluster of high rocks. They clambered up, peering over the edge.

What they saw took their breath away.

In the violet glow, a thousand feet moved in lockstep. Swords rattled and shields clanked, and ragged banners hung limp in the windless air. A dark army was on the march. The soldiers moved with a strange, jerky gait, shuffling along a wide stone causeway that ran across the lakebed. Then the moon emerged from behind a cloud and Alish stifled a cry.

'They're... dead!' she managed, her

face a mask of horror.

She was right. They were deadwalkers, corpses animated by some grim magic, the dry skin stretched like parchment over their emaciated frames. They were led by a tall figure on horseback, a skeletal general, his skull gleaming in the moonlight.

'Move, you stinking bonebags!' he cried, his harsh voice ringing in the stillness.

Behind them came another phalanx of dark shapes – these seemed to drift above the ground, black cloaks flapping raggedly even though there was no wind. They carried pale steel scythes, and beneath their hoods Thanis could see nothing but darkness.

'Nighthaunts from Shyish,' Kaspar whispered. 'The Realm of Death.'

'And that must be their Realmgate,' Kiri said, pointing.

The spectral soldiers had emerged from a huge hole sunk into the bottom of the mere. It lay on an angle, open to the sky – more like a mouth than a cave, Thanis thought, ringed with jagged rocks like great black teeth. The violet light pulsated from inside, making the walls gleam like a huge gullet. The air seemed thick somehow, waves of dark power radiating from within.

'Warpstone,' she realised aloud. It was the same sensation they'd felt in the Skaven warren, as the packlord Kreech revealed his warpstone crystal.

Kiri nodded grimly. 'That whole tunnel

must be made of it. It must be why they drained the lake, to get to the crystal and open the gate.'

'But who?' Alish asked. 'Who would have such power?'

Kiri got to her feet, gritting her teeth. 'That's what we're here to find out. We have to get closer.'

Alish gasped in dismay, and Kaspar shook his head. 'You're mad. There are thousands of them.'

'Kiri's right,' Thanis said. 'Strongstem told us we had to find out who was poisoning his forest. That was his price for healing Elio.'

'So let's go back and tell him what we've seen,' Kaspar hissed. 'He can find a way to come down here and kill whoever it turns out to be.'

'No,' Kiri said. 'Don't you see? It's all connected. This dark army, I'd bet my slingshot they're the same ones besieging Lifestone. And this warpstone looks like the same stuff Kreech was given for taking Vertigan, which means that whoever drained the lake and dug up the crystal also has our master. That person must be here, I'm sure of it. Which means...'

With a lurch, Thanis saw what she was getting at. 'Which means Vertigan could be here too.'

Kiri nodded. 'We have to look. We don't have a choice.'

Kaspar sighed, clutching his chest. 'All right. But don't say I didn't warn you.'

CHAPTER SIX

Ashnakh

They scrambled down a shelf of rock
and crouched in the shadows. Between
them and that giant rocky maw the
ground was scattered with scree and
boulders. But the moon was bright
and the warpstone glow filled the air,
pulsating from the cavern.

'Kaspar, which way?' Kiri asked.

He frowned, pointing. 'That big rock
ought to hide us. But we need to stay
low, and move fast.'

Thanis squeezed his shoulder. 'The
realm's best sneak,' she said, and he
smiled worriedly.

Kaspar led the way and Thanis and

the others followed, ducking through the maze of boulders towards the tall, jagged rock. They huddled behind it, barely daring to breathe. Kaspar peered round the edge.

'I think we can make it down to that pile of stones,' he gestured. 'From there we should be able to see–'

There was a crunch nearby and he clamped his mouth shut. The sound came again – footsteps, drawing closer. Then a voice rang out, and they shrank back into the boulder's shadow.

'Anything moving?' it said, a dry, icy rasp that made Thanis shiver.

More footsteps approached. 'Nothing,' a feminine voice replied, as cold and lifeless as the first. 'This place is deader than Shyish.'

'What I do not understand,' the first voice said, 'is why the mistress feels the need to bring in more of these filthy corpses. We could overrun that feeble city in half a day. Why does she delay?'

The female hissed. 'It is not your place to question Ashnakh. She will attack when she is ready.'

'I think there's something there that she needs,' the other mused. 'Something within Lifestone that is important to her. We could take it for ourselves, and...'

Thanis heard a thud and a scuffle. 'One more word and I will turn you to dust. Do not question the mistress. Now come, there's no one out here.'

They moved away, their boots crunching on the scree. Kaspar leaned out, Kiri and Thanis watching over his shoulder. The figures were heavily armoured, dark hair hanging over their broad shoulders. They had pale skin, and wore long red cloaks.

'Soulblights,' Kaspar whispered when they were out of sight. 'Undead bloodsuckers. This just gets better.'

Thanis frowned at him. 'How do you know so much about all these... dead things?'

Kaspar hesitated for a moment, then he exposed the mark on his wrist. 'After Vertigan told me I was marked for Shyish, I asked him what kind of place it was. I soon wished I hadn't. He told me all about Nagash, the Lord of Death, about the nighthaunts with their frightful touch, and the soulblight vampires who prey on the living. They must be acting as sentries for... whoever's behind this.'

'Um, I think I might know who that is,' Alish said. 'Look.'

She pointed and Thanis lifted her head, gazing up past the boulder, past the shuffling army.

Yes, she thought. *That's who we've been looking for.*

The figure hung in mid-air, suspended in the mouth of the warpstone tunnel. Her eyes were closed and her skin seemed to glow from within, a light that pulsated with the waves of power flowing from the walls of crystal. Shapes moved around her, limbless spectres with red eyes and nebulous bodies, holding her aloft. She seemed to be feeding on the warpstone, streams of energy flowing into the tips of her fingers.

Kaspar shuddered, shrinking back. But Kiri was nodding, her eyes wide.

'That's her. That night in Lifestone when Vertigan came after me, the night he was taken, she was there. She's the hooded lady.'

'Did Vertigan tell you anything about her?' Thanis asked.

Kiri shook her head. 'No, he wouldn't. He said it was too soon or something. But they knew each other from old times. And he did tell me she was dangerous. He was very clear on that.'

'And he was right,' a voice said, and they looked up.

The hooded lady's eyes were open, shafts of purple energy slanting from them like light through clouds. She was a long way off but her voice was somehow close, as though she was speaking inside their heads.

'Welcome, all of you,' she said, giving the most chilling smile Thanis had ever seen. 'I've been so looking forward to this.'

Slowly she began to float down towards them, the army passing beneath her feet, those formless shapes coiling around her body. Thanis wanted to pull away, to hide or to run, but she found herself frozen. She glanced at the others – they, too, were pinned in place, staring helplessly.

'I am the sorceress Ashnakh,' the woman said. 'Do not trouble to introduce yourselves, your names are known to me. Kiri, the outsider. Alish, the inventor. Thanis, the fighter. Kaspar, the thief.' She looked at each of them in turn, pausing for a moment on Kaspar's face. 'I also know of the marks you each bear, and the reason your master brought you together.'

Thanis fought against the binding spell, sweat pouring down her face.

By sheer force of will she managed to raise Vertigan's staff. 'You know who this belonged to,' she said, pushing the words out. 'You took our master. Give him back!'

The sorceress tilted her head. 'You're a brave little thing, aren't you? Trust me, you shouldn't start a fight you have no way of winning.'

Thanis gritted her teeth. 'We'll find Vertigan,' she managed. 'And he will destroy you.'

With a surge of effort she reached out, grasping Kiri by the arm. Immediately she felt the spell weaken, her own strength returning. Kiri reached for Alish, moving as though underwater, fighting the sorceress for every inch. Then her hand locked around the girl's birthmark and the three of them were joined.

Thanis turned to Kaspar, nodding to her arm. 'Take it,' she said. 'We need you too.'

But he just looked at her, his eyes

wide beneath his hood. 'I can't,' he said. 'I'm too afraid.'

'And you are right to be,' Ashnakh growled, staring furiously down at them. She clasped her hands together and Thanis saw light inside them, a ball of energy growing between her fingers. She turned her hands and the power exploded outwards, a ball of fire blazing through the night air. It bore the image of a screaming skull, mouth wide and howling as it streaked towards them.

Thanis felt their combined power gather in her veins, and directed it into Vertigan's staff. She brought it up and the fireball impacted against it, shattering into a thousand tattered fragments. From the tip of the staff a light blazed, a blinding whiteness edged with violet, as though it had absorbed the fireball's power and turned it back, sending it blazing into the night air.

The sorceress gasped, shielding her eyes. The wraiths surrounding her

howled and shrieked, forced back by the
light flaring from the staff.

Then it was gone, and so was
Ashnakh, driven away towards the cave.

Thanis let go of Kiri's arm. She
looked at the staff in amazement. 'I
didn't know it could do that.'

Kiri grinned. 'Now let's go. We've seen
what we needed to see.'

But Kaspar still stood frozen, staring
down into the bottom of the lake.
Following his gaze, Thanis felt her
blood freeze.

Complete silence had fallen. The

army of the dead had ceased marching. Instead they stood facing back up the rise, countless empty eye sockets turned in the children's direction.

The deadwalkers took a step in unison, then another. Then they raised their arms and broke formation, shuffling with surprising speed over the uneven ground.

Thanis grabbed Kaspar's arm. 'Run!'

CHAPTER SEVEN

Tentacles

As they scrambled across open ground they could hear the dark army pursuing them, the deadwalkers moaning as they came. Thanis grabbed Alish, hoisting the girl onto her shoulders.

'I'm okay!' she protested. 'I can run.'

'I know,' Thanis said. 'But I can run faster.'

They broke around the tumble of high rocks, struggling through a sump of clinging mud. The deadwalkers were gaining, moving in shuffling gangs to cut them off. Kiri slipped, splashing down, but Kaspar hoisted her to her feet and they kept running. His eyes were filled with a wild fear that Thanis had never seen before, and she wondered why he'd refused to take her wrist, why the sorceress's eyes had lingered on his face. But there was no time to think about it now.

She felt bony fingers clutching at her sleeve: a deadwalker was veering towards her, trying to pull her down. She drove the staff into its torso and it fell on its backside, one leg detaching and rolling into the mire. But more of the creatures were advancing on all sides, led by the skeletal warrior on his fleshless horse.

'After them, you measly rotsacks!' he cried out. 'For Ashnakh!'

He dug in his spurs and the dead horse whinnied, charging through the mud towards them. Kiri loosed a shot

from her catapult but it was no use – the pellet simply lodged in the warrior's ribcage. He lifted his blade, cackling as he thundered closer.

'Foolish creature! You think you can stand against the might of Ashnakh and her army of the dead? You will learn the error of your– aaargh!'

Suddenly he flew up into the air, the whip tumbling from his hand. Thanis stared in surprise as he howled and swiped, trying to grab his own ankle. Wrapped around it was a pale, bulbous tentacle, swinging him from side to side as he wailed and cursed. For a moment she thought it was another one of those foul creepers, then she saw what it was attached to.

The leviathan was awake, a purple

gleam shining in its hideous black eyes. Its tail flapped, sending up fountains of mud. Its tentacles writhed like a nest of snakes. The skeletal general swung towards its yawning mouth, a rank black hole ringed with rows of chitinous yellow teeth. The tentacle let go and he dropped inside. There was a crunch like a dog chewing bones.

Hearing a cry, Thanis whipped round. Kaspar lay on his back, looking up at her in terror. One of the tentacles had hold of him and was dragging him away through the mud. Thanis lifted Alish off her shoulders. 'Stay here,' she said firmly, raising the staff as she charged towards the beast.

She took hold of Kaspar's arm and it became a tug of war, the boy howling as Thanis and the tentacle tested each other's strength. But she knew the creature would never release him – Kaspar would be pulled in half first. She swung the staff right and left, and heard one, two, three moist thuds.

Hearing a scream, she looked back. Alish was surrounded by a horde of deadwalkers, swinging her hammer to drive them back. Kiri was with her, catapult raised. Thanis wanted to run to them but she couldn't – one battle at a time, and right now she had to save Kaspar.

She dropped the staff. The tentacles were writhing above her head. Locating the one that had snatched Kaspar she gripped it with her steel gloves, squeezing as hard as she could. The tentacle began to writhe more violently, yanking the boy higher. He wailed, swinging towards that toothy maw.

The skin of the tentacle broke and Thanis felt her steel-clad fingers digging in, and then black ichor was bubbling to the surface, splattering her. She gave a tug and a twist and the tentacle tore in half, spewing foul black liquid. Thanis felt it spray across her face, and she recoiled in disgust.

She held out her arms and Kaspar dropped into them, his eyes wide with shock. 'Caught you again,' Thanis said, but he could only whimper and wipe his face.

Kiri and Alish stood inside a ring of bodies, defending themselves as the deadwalkers advanced. Thanis dropped Kaspar, grabbing the staff, and together they drove through the mass of corpses. The deadwalkers snapped at them, biting and lunging, but Thanis forced them back, swinging with the staff. More tentacles came lashing towards them, but their twitching ends found the arms and ankles of the zombie soldiers, lifting them off the ground. Blank eyes stared haplessly as they swung through the air, and Thanis heard that revolting crunch again.

She lifted Alish up, and looked around. The leviathan had cleared a path through the deadwalkers so they made for it, dodging the tentacles, their boots crunching as they regained solid ground.

They sprinted past the sunken ship, kicking through the graveyard of sailors' bones. Some of them were rising from their graves, tottering to their feet and turning on the children as they ducked through. Thanis felt the lakebed begin to slope upwards, and in the moonlight she saw the old riverbed, emptying into the dry lake. But the corpses were closing in, and as they reached the river she dared to glance back. As far as she could see, every patch of open ground was covered with the undead, swarming madly in their direction. In the distance, a dark shape rose over the lake – Ashnakh had recovered herself and was drifting through the air towards them, energy boiling between her hands.

'It's no use,' Kaspar said. 'She's too strong. Those things will run us down long before we reach Strongstem.'

Thanis gritted her teeth. Deep down she knew he was right.

Then she remembered something.

'Alish,' she said, lifting the girl from her shoulders. 'Give me your hammer. I've got an idea.'

Ahead of them loomed the great dam

and the mounds of earth, humped and silent in the darkness. Thanis took the hammer from Alish and ran to the wall of wood. The planks were bending outwards with the strain of containing the water which roared within. Summoning every ounce of muscle she swung the hammer, aiming for one of the heavy stanchions that kept the dam in place. The wood shook, but did not move. Thanis swung again, screaming with effort, and this time she heard a deep, creaking groan. By now Kiri had stepped in to help, smacking on the stanchions with a length of wood. Alish wielded a rock, slamming it into the planks. But the corpses were drawing closer, shuffling towards them.

Finally, there was a snap and one of the supports fell, striking the soft ground. Thanis heaved the hammer and another limb snapped, the wall bowing outwards, the planks straining to hold back the river. 'Get back, all of you!' she cried. 'It's going to go!'

CHAPTER EIGHT

Dire Wolves

They leapt clear, sprinting up a high
mound of earth. There was a deep,
unearthly creak and a thunder of pops
and cracks, then the dam broke at last.

The Everlight River burst free in
a glittering wave, smashing through
the wooden bulwark and driving the
corpse legions with it. It seemed to
roar almost joyfully, breakers crashing
as the water reclaimed its old course.
Their heap of earth became an island,
the water gushing into the lake,
deadwalkers rolling in the surf.

Thanis handed Alish back her
hammer. The girl was staring up at her
in wonder.

'That was amazing,' she said.

Thanis blushed. 'Thanks.'

There was a sudden hiss in the distance, as though a thousand fires had been doused simultaneously by a thousand buckets of water. Looking back Thanis saw a plume of steam rolling into the air, lit by shafts of purple light. Violet beams pierced the clouds and there was a scream of absolute frustration, echoing from the shores of the lake and the hills beyond.

At first she didn't know what was happening, then she realised. The water must have reached the warpstone tunnel, flooding inside. Ashnakh had broken off her pursuit, her distant figure retreating, her enraged howls resounding across the scarred land.

Kiri grinned. 'I think we made her mad.'

They waded through shallow water back to the riverbank, heading upstream. Their way was lit by the

glow from the Everlight River as
they struggled over rocks and shingle,
through patches of clinging moss
and chattering reeds. Nesting birds
squawked angrily, flapping away on
bent silver wings. Toads croaked and
gurgled in the swampy patches, and
one of them spat a foul substance that
struck Thanis's breastplate dead centre,
hissing like acid on the metal.

'I've been trying to remember
anything else Vertigan might have said
about Ashnakh,' Kiri said as they ran.
'Anything that could help us fight her.
But it's all so hazy.' She looked back
at Kaspar. 'Wait, do you still have that
stone she gave you? The pyramid?'

Kaspar hesitated, then he reached
inside his tunic and drew out the cord.
Dangling from it was the tiny black
pyramid with the white stone in the
centre. *So I was right*, Thanis thought.
*That's what he's been playing with so
restlessly, all this time.*

'I think you should get rid of it,' she

told him. 'It could be... I don't know, dangerous.'

'It's just a stone,' Kaspar said. 'I've grown sort of fond of it, I...'

'That woman is evil,' Kiri said. 'Any gift from her is not worth keeping.'

'She's right,' Thanis said, suddenly desperate to get the black stone away from Kaspar, away from all of them. 'Ashnakh is powerful, you don't know what she might be able to do. Throw it in the river.'

Kaspar flinched, and for a moment she thought he was going to refuse. Then he shrugged and slipped the cord over his head, clutching the pyramid in his clenched fist. Drawing back he tossed the stone into the glistening water; Thanis heard a quiet *glup*, then Kaspar turned away and kept running.

The ground was rising on either side now, the valley steep and narrow. Kiri slowed, kneeling to inspect a patch of squelchy ground.

'That's Alish's footprint. And there, that one's mine.'

'How do you know?' Alish asked. 'They just look like different bits of mud.'

'Spend enough time in the wilderness, you learn these things,' Kiri said. 'I remember that leaning tree as well, and those two boulders in the river – they look sort of like sleeping troggoths. But look, something else has been here. This branch is broken and that looks like a hoofprint.'

'A horse?' Kaspar asked.

Kiri shook her head. 'Bigger. Look how deep these impressions are.'

Alish shuddered. 'I bet it was that griffon. Did you see its eyes? It had that purple glow in them, just like the river monster and all those deadwalkers. They're all her creatures.'

Kiri frowned. 'And if she's too busy dealing with the flood...'

'She might send them after us,' Kaspar finished for her.

As if on cue, there was a snap in

the undergrowth. They turned as one, bunching together.

'We have to get back to Strongstem,' Thanis said. 'Right now.'

With a roar the bushes broke and a muscled shape sprang towards them. Alish screamed and Thanis pushed her back, sidestepping as a dire wolf bounded past her. It turned, and in its black eyes she saw the same violet gleam.

'This way!' Kiri shouted. 'Come on!'

They ran and the wolf came after them, its paws tearing up the mud. Thanis heard its dry breath and jabbed backwards with the staff, landing a lucky blow across the wolf's snout that sent it reeling and whining. They reached the trees, struggling over buried roots and through slippery leaves. The dire wolf came on again, and now Thanis saw that it had friends – two more loping shapes, their fangs bared as they bounded up the slope.

Higher up the ground had been washed out in a rainstorm; a tree lay on its side, roots exposed. Beyond it the soil was loose and rocky, and they had to crouch and pull themselves up. As he reached the top Kaspar slowed, lashing out with his heels and sending loose rocks and earth toppling back down. Thanis followed his lead, kicking a decent-sized boulder and watching it tumble down the hillside. One of the dire wolves tried to spring clear, lost its footing and tumbled back into the tangle of trees. The other two shied away, their paws scrabbling.

Thanis could see the top of the rise now, black against the moonlit sky. Just a little further, and they'd be safe. Then she heard a cry from above that made her blood freeze.

A huge shape circled, blocking out the stars. 'The griffon!' Alish screamed as the beast folded its wings and plunged, giving another heart-stopping shriek as it crashed through the canopy of trees. Kiri dropped and rolled, pulling Alish with her. The griffon shouldered through the branches, gripping with its talons and snapping down at them. Kiri loaded her catapult with fumbling fingers, dropped her shot then loaded again, taking aim as the creature's beak sliced like a sword.

She loosed just as it opened its mouth, her pellet disappearing inside. The griffon's eyes widened and it began to hack and splutter, gobbets of filthy phlegm flying out. It shook its head furiously, taking to the air with a hoarse croak. Kiri jumped up, Alish on her heels.

More dark shapes swooped in and Thanis felt something peck at her hair, its black feathers swiping as she lashed out with her steel glove. The raven rose, rejoining the flock that spiralled overhead, black against the moon's white face. Then they burst through a last wall of trees to the top of the ridge.

'Strongstem!' Alish cried. 'Strongstem, we're back, we're–' She stopped in confusion. The three Sylvaneth still stood, motionless, but there was no sign of Strongstem. 'He's gone. He left us!'

The griffon keened, its shadow racing across the stony ground. The wolves loped onto the ridge – there were more than ever now, a rangy, ragged pack, their eyes shining like sparks of warpstone. Ravens landed in the exposed branches, watching them silently. For a moment all was still.

Then another shape rose from the valley, drifting soundlessly towards them. Countless spirits wreathed around Ashnakh's body as she floated above the treetops, shielding her and keeping her aloft. Her eyes shone with fury and around her clenched fists Thanis saw coils of purple energy.

Thanis raised the staff but Ashnakh snarled, shaking her head.

'It won't help you this time,' she

spat. 'No more surprises. I'll admit, I underestimated you children. And now I'll have to start again damming that foul river, emptying that disgusting lake, raising more deadwalker slaves.'

'We told you to give Vertigan back,' Thanis said. 'We warned you what would happen.'

The sorceress's eyes narrowed. 'Very well, if you insist. You can have him.'

Kiri frowned in surprise. 'R-really?'

Ashnakh smiled. 'Of course. Come with me to Shyish, to my Palace of Mirrors, and you can be reunited with him.'

Thanis curled her lip. 'We're not going anywhere with you. Give him to us, here and now, or go and leave us alone.'

The sorceress gestured to the creatures surrounding them – the hunched and waiting wolves, the patient ravens, the circling griffon. They began to close in, forcing the four of them back.

'You can't kill us,' Kaspar stammered.

'You need us for something. You need our birthmarks.'

Ashnakh smiled. 'That's true. But it doesn't mean I need you intact. An eye here, a limb there, it makes no difference. And one way or another, you're coming with me.'

The ravens took silently to the air, a vortex of black wings. The wolves sprang up, their jaws dripping with slaver. The griffon plunged through the sky, claws bared, twin beaks yammering. Ashnakh drifted closer,

raising her head and laughing, a cold, cackling sound that rang through the still night air.

Thanis gripped Alish's arm and knew they didn't stand a chance.

CHAPTER NINE

A Child of Lifestone

They retreated along the ridge towards
the three frozen Sylvaneth. The
tree-people stood sentinel, motionless
and staring as the wolves advanced.
Thanis looked again. She was sure
their eyes had been closed before. Now
they gleamed dully in the moonlight.

Suddenly, she felt a sharp pain in
her shoulder. She looked down and the
spite stared back, moonlight reflected in
its many-faceted eyes. She was about to
swipe it away when she realised. If the
spite was here, that could only mean...

With a roar, Strongstem burst onto
the ridge, his great fists raised. Spites

darted around his mighty crown, whining like a swarm of spike-hornets. Litheroot strode at his side, her eyes bright with green fire. She gave a fierce battle cry, the earth shaking with the force of it.

A line of tree-revenants advanced into the open, swinging scythes with polished blades that made the air thrum. They came on stride by stride, an unstoppable wall of wood and will. Thanis felt her breath catch – there was such grace in their movements, such relentless power. It was as though everything that terrified her about the natural world – its strangeness, its ferocity, its sheer, unknowable purpose – had been given form and movement.

The dire wolves sprang, two of them leaping at Strongstem, fangs bared. He batted them away without slowing and they crashed to the soil, tangled and snarling. The ravens rounded on Litheroot, beaks snapping at her eyes. She raised her arms and a storm of leaves swept upwards, spiralling like a hurricane, scattering the ravens in every direction.

Then there was a *whump* and one of the tree-revenants burst into purple fire, batting desperately at its upper branches. Ashnakh loosed another skull-headed fireball and the ground in front of Strongstem erupted, throwing him back. At the same moment the griffon swooped, claws tearing at his uppermost branches, trying to lift the treelord off the ground.

Before she knew what she was doing, Thanis was running in. She gripped the staff, swiping at the griffon with all her might. Her first blow caught it under the wing. Her next slammed into its left-side beak, and she felt the impact down to her bones. The creature turned, cawing furiously, and Strongstem used the distraction to reach upwards, grasping the griffon around the right-side neck and slamming its head into the floor. He spread his free hand wide and roots burst from his fingertips, coiling around the struggling creature, binding its wings and burying themselves in the earth, holding it down. The griffon fought and kicked but this time it could not break free.

'I will not kill it,' Strongstem told Thanis. 'It was once noble and proud, and may be again once this poison has been washed from our lands. Once this ancient forest is pure again.'

In that moment she felt a strange realisation. Yes, the Sylvaneth were terrifying – a force of nature in the purest sense. But they had to be: to protect what was theirs, to ensure that the natural world endured, that it did not become corrupted and overrun. She'd always been frightened of the world outside the city, and now she knew she was right to be – life out here was tough, and relentless, and unreasoning. But it was beautiful too, and worth fighting for. If she'd never left her home, if she'd never taken this risk, she'd never have known that.

Turning, she reached for Alish, grabbing her wrist. She felt the power again, radiating up through her arm and deep into her heart. Kiri took hold of her and it intensified; Thanis almost laughed with the thrill of it. She gestured to Kaspar and for a moment he hesitated. Then his eyes locked on hers and he extended his wrist to Alish.

They turned to face the approaching threat, faces bright in the moonlight.

Then another hand locked around
Kiri's wrist, holding on tight. Elio stood
beside her, his cheeks flushed.

'You're healed!' Alish cried. There was
a white scar on his forehead, but the
burn itself had vanished.

'Thanks to Litheroot,' Elio said. 'I
don't know what they did to me, I feel
like I've been away a long time. But I
feel stronger than ever.'

Kiri squinted at him. 'Your eyes! I
could swear they used to be brown.'

Elio grinned. His eyes were the green

of grass, of trees, of Ghyran itself. 'I'll tell you all about it when we're not about to get eaten by wolves.'

They broke apart, turning to face the creatures closing around them. Thanis could feel the strength flowing through her, radiating from her mark. How it worked, she had no idea; it was enough to know that it did. Alish swung her hammer and Kiri wielded her catapult; Kaspar grabbed a length of sturdy wood and Thanis tossed Vertigan's staff to Elio, watching as he caught it and swung it around, smashing three ravens out of the sky. A wolf sprang towards Thanis but she barely flinched, raising her gloves like a boxer. As it drew closer she ducked and swung, striking the creature square on the nose. It turned tail and ran, whining, into the trees.

Looking around she could see the other dire wolves doing the same, and the ravens fleeing into the cloudless sky. The griffon lay bound, no longer struggling. Ashnakh gave a cry of impotent anger as Strongstem drew himself up, facing her.

'Begone, servant of Nagash,' he said. 'Take your foul creatures and your vile poisons and leave this place.'

The sorceress sneered. 'Pitiful shrub, do not challenge me. You do not know who you are dealing with.'

'But I do,' Litheroot said, stepping up beside the treelord. 'I know more than you think, Ashnakh of Shyish. Or should I say Aisha of Lifestone?'

The sorceress blanched, her lips tightening bitterly. 'Where did you hear that name?'

Litheroot smiled, her eyes shining. 'From the lips of a dying man. A man I fought to save, though it cost me dearly.'

Ashnakh nodded, the wraiths circling her body. 'I always wondered who saved Vertigan's pitiful life. You shall pay for that mistake with your own!'

And she unleashed a barrage of

searing energy, streams of violet light
bursting from her open palms. The
spectres coiled around her wrists,
adding their strength to hers, the light
screaming as it descended on Litheroot.

But the branchwych was ready.
She flung up her arms, a screen of
living branches shielding her from
the sorceress's attack. Then she let
loose a volley of her own, a wave
of shimmering thorns streaking like
arrows through the air. Ashnakh waved
a hand and the thorns dispersed,
scattering to the winds. But one caught
her on the wrist, drawing the faintest
red scratch.

The sorceress cursed, her eyes
flashing. Then she looked down at
Thanis and the others, the spirits
wreathing round her body. 'You know
where to find the one you seek,' she
said. 'In the Palace of Mirrors, in the
realm of Shyish. Come for him, if you
dare.'

Then she turned away, the wraiths

howling as she retreated into the night. Thanis saw her outlined against the gleaming band of the river far below, then she was gone.

Litheroot shivered. 'That is a creature of death,' she said. 'She has no place in the Realm of Life.'

Strongstem gave a grumble of assent. 'But she was of Ghyran once. I felt the pulse of life deep within her, though it has become corrupted. Just as she corrupted this forest.' He lowered his head, looking down at the children. 'I am sorry I was not here to greet you. The dark power was too great, I was forced to retreat.'

'And what about now?' Alish asked. 'How were you able to fight?'

'It has waned,' Strongstem said. 'It is not gone, but it is weaker. This was your doing, and for it I offer my thanks. We will double our efforts, and drive this poison back where it came from.'

'How did you know about Vertigan?'

Kaspar asked, turning to Litheroot. 'And what did you mean, you saved his life?'

The branchwych smiled. 'Elio told me all about your master, and your quest to bring him home. Don't resent him for it, Kaspar. He decided to trust me and he was right to do so. We Sylvaneth may guard our lands and our secrets jealously, but in this great war we are all on the same side.

'My meeting with Vertigan took place a long time ago. As I said, he was dying, the result of a terrible mystical injury. The healers at the Arbour didn't know how to treat him, so they sought us out. In those days this was not so rare – relations between the city and the Sylvaneth were... perhaps not good, but better than today. When I saw his wounds and recognised the dark magics that had been used to inflict them, I agreed to try and heal him.'

'So we made the same journey Vertigan did,' Thanis said. 'We came to you for help, just like him.' Somehow this knowledge gave her hope, as though they were on the right trail.

Litheroot nodded. 'He was in far more danger than Elio. It took many moons to bring him back, to find the soul inhabiting his battered body. In that time he spoke a great deal, often senselessly, sometimes with clarity. And there was one name he repeated, over and over, like a litany.'

'Aisha,' Kiri guessed. 'But who was she?'

'She was the girl he loved,' Litheroot said sadly. 'And she betrayed him, utterly and terribly. She killed his friends, she tore his world to pieces – she almost destroyed him, too. His heart was broken, and his spirit with it. I do not know how it happened, all I know is there was a ritual, and a fountain... To learn the full story you would have to ask Vertigan himself.'

'So we have to go to Shyish,' Thanis said. 'We have to find this Palace of Mirrors and bring him home.'

'I would not advise that,' Strongstem said. 'You may be brave, but the Realm of Death is no place for children. You should return to Lifestone and stay out of trouble.'

'We can't,' Kiri argued. 'Vertigan wouldn't stop searching for us.'

'Is there anything you can tell us?' Kaspar asked. 'Anything that could help defeat Ashnakh?'

Litheroot considered this. 'There is one thing you should not forget. She was human once, a child like you. She too was born in Lifestone, the city raised her. If you could find the place where she grew up, the house she called home, then perhaps you could learn something that could help you. Some knowledge you could use against her.'

'But Lifestone is huge,' Kaspar said. 'How are we supposed to find one house in a whole city?'

For a moment there was silence, then Elio sighed. 'The lord's scribes keep records of everyone who ever lived inside the walls. If I asked my father, I could probably find out where this Aisha grew up.'

'You'd do that?' Thanis asked. 'Talk to your father, I mean?'

'It doesn't sound like I have a choice,' Elio said. 'If we can learn something, it'll be worth it.'

Kiri nodded. 'Now all we have to do is find that flying deathtrap and hope it still works.'

Alish scowled. 'It'll work,' she said defensively. 'Well, probably.'

CHAPTER TEN

The Sky-Beast

Alish twisted cogs frantically as the
Arbour Seed lifted unsteadily off the
ground, straining against the pull
of gravity. Thanis leaned over the
railing, waving down at Strongstem
and Litheroot as their sturdy forms
dwindled among the surrounding trees.
She blinked, and when she looked again
they had vanished, blending back into
the forest as though they were never
there at all.

The land was a rolling emerald
blanket under the clear morning sky,
the rising sun driving the mist from
the hollows and sparkling on the

ribbon of the Everlight River. It looked peaceful, but Thanis knew this was an illusion – there was danger down there, and struggle, and fierce, forceful life. 'But I'm not scared any more,' she whispered.

Kaspar tipped his head towards her. 'Not scared of what?'

'Of... all this,' Thanis said. 'I used to think nature was out to get me. That if I left the city I'd be eaten by a dire wolf or strangled by a creeper-vine or squashed by a Sylvaneth.'

Kaspar frowned. 'Literally all of those things nearly happened to us.'

Thanis laughed. 'But we survived, didn't we? There's danger everywhere you go. The trick is to try and understand it, so it feels less terrifying. Oh, I don't know what I'm trying to say.'

'I do,' Kaspar said, his hand straying instinctively towards his throat. 'I think I do.'

Thanis watched him, doubt still gnawing at her heart. He'd thrown the pyramid away, hadn't he? So why was his hand still brushing against his chest, as though... An image flashed into her mind, of a coin sparkling as Kaspar pulled it from behind her ear. A little sleight-of-hand trick, a moment of illusion. Could it be possible?

Then Alish cried out, 'Lifestone ahoy!'

Thanis turned. The mountain peaks rose sheer in the distance, shelf upon shelf to the high horizon. The city nestled at their feet, a pale smudge among the grey foothills. But as they drew closer she could see a dark mist surrounding it, a pall of smoke blanketing the valley.

'What if they've already attacked?' she wondered aloud. 'What if the city's already fallen?'

'Remember what those soulblights were saying,' Kaspar said. 'Ashnakh won't attack until she has something she needs. Maybe it's the sixth mark.'

'Scratch,' Thanis said, remembering the ragged boy in the Skaven warren. 'We should get to him first. But how?'

Kiri frowned. 'We'll think of something. First we should find Aisha's house, like Litheroot said. We have to talk to Lord Elias.'

Elio blanched, gripping the railing. 'Oh, this is not going to be fun.'

They soared closer and now they could see the dark army camped outside the city walls, still waiting. Their ranks had swelled, reinforcements marching from the Realmgate at Rawdeep Mere. If she stilled her breath Thanis could hear their footsteps, a steady drumbeat echoing in the trees.

'Here come the ravens,' Kiri said, loading her catapult. The birds flocked towards them, plunging through the haze of smoke. Thanis hefted the staff, ready to strike.

Then something hit the gondola and the airship tilted violently, ropes creaking as they lost altitude.

'They're shooting at us!' Kaspar said. 'Alish, quick, take us up.'

He was right – the skeletal soldiers
were loosing arrows and hurling rocks,
though they were too far below to
make contact. But there in the baying
mob was a huge brute, a deadwalker
so tall and broad he must have been
a troggoth or even a gargant when
he was alive. He carried a catapult
ten times the size of Kiri's, and they
watched him snatch up a boulder and
load it into the cradle.

The rock glanced off the base of
the airship, splintering the wood and
falling back, burying three regular-sized

deadwalkers when it smashed into the ground. The huge zombie loaded again, but by now they were rising, Alish working quickly to lift them out of range. The creature's next shot passed under them.

'You missed!' Thanis shouted.

'But that won't,' Kaspar said, and pointed.

On the far side of the sprawling encampment was a line of siege engines – huge trebuchets made from hacked-down trees, lashed together with lengths of rope. As Thanis watched, one of them was wheeled forwards by a host of deadwalkers and loaded with lumps of stone and iron, a barrage of shot that would pummel the *Arbour Seed* to pieces. A pair of armoured soulblights wound the winch tight, angling the catapult towards the airship. One drew his sword, preparing to cut the rope.

'Up, Alish,' Thanis urged. 'As high as you can.'

'But we'll overshoot the city,' Alish protested. 'We'll have to turn around and—'

'None of that matters!' Kiri shouted. 'Take us up, now!'

There was a twang as the catapult loosed, ten tons of rock and metal hurtling towards them. Alish worked desperately, twisting cogs as the ravens flapped and cawed around her. The balloon billowed as the *Arbour Seed* lifted towards the clouds, ropes straining.

The debris from the catapult whistled beneath them, a great cry going up as it fell back to earth, flattening a whole platoon of corpses. Then the clouds consumed them, the city and the ravens and the great dead army all disappearing in the fog.

'We're still climbing,' Alish said. 'We need to get down again, I just... What's that?'

Something was sparkling in the clouds, a ribbon of glittering energy like a seam of gold in rock. They drifted closer, staring in wonder as it shifted and shone, a shimmering pattern of crystals or droplets, Thanis couldn't quite tell. Now they were almost touching it, the airship gliding through the mysterious substance. There was an inflow pipe on the port side, sucking in air to feed the steam-bellows. Some of the substance spiralled in, and for a moment the pipes glowed golden.

Then, like a bullet fired from a musket, the airship shot upwards, the clouds breaking around them as they rose in a vertical line. Thanis grabbed the railing, hearing Alish cry out as the *Arbour Seed* ascended, the wood shaking and the balloon bulging outwards.

'What's happening?' Kiri shouted over the howl of the wind.

'I don't know!' Alish admitted. 'That shiny stuff must've got into the pipes.'

They broke into bright sunlight, the clouds a dense carpet below them, only the highest mountain peaks poking through. The air was so cold that it burned Thanis's lungs; she found herself fighting for breath, and saw Kaspar and Elio doing the same. Kiri wrapped her scarf around her face, ice crystals forming in her lashes.

Then Alish found the right gauge and their ascent slowed, the airship tracking an arc through the blue sky. They drifted down and soon they could breathe again, the air around them warming.

'Do you think that's the stuff the Kharadron use?' Alish wondered. 'The thing that makes their airships fly?'

'It could be,' Kiri said. 'Just try not to fly through any more of it on the way back down, we don't want to go that fast in the opposite direction.'

'Um, I don't think we're alone up here,' Kaspar said, pointing. 'I see... something.'

A dark shape moved between the mountains, weaving just above the cloud layer. As the *Arbour Seed* descended it disappeared, dipping into the clouds like a sea creature sinking beneath the waves.

'What was it?' Elio asked. 'Some kind of drake, or–'

The shape rose once more, and now they could see it clearly. Kaspar gripped Thanis's hand, and she heard herself whimper. The sky-beast was covered from head to tail in dense blue fur, rippling in waves along its back. It didn't seem to have wings, and she wondered how it could stay up – perhaps it fed on the same substance they had just encountered, the stuff that kept airships afloat. She wondered if that was its entire diet, or if it liked more solid food, too.

Moments later, she had her answer. The creature came towards them and opened its massive mouth, exposing rows of teeth the size of buildings. Its claws were red and razor-sharp, swiping at the air.

Kiri drew her catapult, taking careful aim. Thanis almost laughed – a shot from her would be less than a gnat's bite to this monster, like flicking a grain of sand at a giant. Then Kiri loosed and the shot was true, flying right towards the sky-beast's moonlike eye.

The pellet struck the milky membrane and the creature roared, blinking furiously. It angled away from them, reaching up with one huge paw to scratch at its eyelid. Just a grain of sand, Thanis thought, but in the right place it can still be painful.

'I'm taking us down,' Alish said, peering over the side as the clouds rushed up to meet them. The beast howled again, making the gondola vibrate. Thanis held on tight as the fog wrapped around them, hiding the beast from view. She breathed a sigh of relief. That had been much too close.

Then a shadow moved in the mist and they heard that deep cry again.

They looked at one another as they plummeted through the clinging clouds. Thanis saw darkness moving and heard the sound of rushing air. *It's hunting for us*, she realised. *It hasn't given up*.

Suddenly the clouds broke, and she saw that black maw yawning open as the sky-beast soared in, vast and unstoppable. Huge teeth passed by on either side, the jaws closing over them.

Darkness descended as the *Arbour Seed* was swallowed whole.

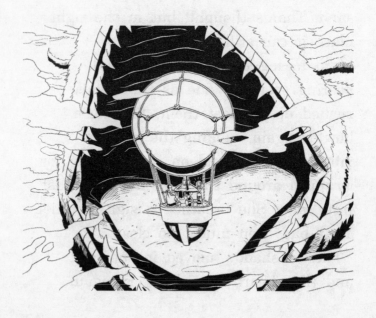

REALMS ARCANA

PART THREE

THE MORTAL REALMS

Each of the Mortal Realms is a world
unto itself, steeped in powerful magic.
Seemingly infinite in size, they contain
limitless possibilities for discovery and
adventure: floating cities and enchanted
woodlands, noble beings and dread
beasts beyond imagination. But in every
corner of every realm, a war rages
between the armies of Order and the
forces of Chaos. This centuries-long
conflict must be won if the realms are
to live in peace and freedom.

AZYR

The Realm of
Heavens, where
the immortal King
Sigmar reigns
unchallenged.

AQSHY

The Realm of Fire,
a region of mighty
volcanoes, molten
seas and flaming-hot
tempers.

GHYRAN

The Realm of Life,
where flourishing
forests teem with
creatures beyond
counting.

CHAMON

The Realm of
Metal, where rivers
of mercury flow
through canyons of
steel.

SHYISH

The Realm of Death, a lifeless land where spirits drift through silent, shaded tombs.

GHUR

The Realm of Beasts, where living monstrosities battle for dominance.

HYSH

The Realm of Light, where knowledge and wisdom are prized above all.

ULGU

The Realm of Shadows, a domain of darkness where dread phantoms lurk.

GHYRAN

Ghyran is the Realm of Life, a flourishing wilderness where the spirit of nature dominates. From rolling grass plains to dense forests, mountain meadows to overgrown cities, every corner of Ghyran is teeming with living things, many of them wild, unpredictable and dangerous. The realm is also a battleground, where the armies of King Sigmar and the Lady Alarielle have fought some of their fiercest campaigns against the forces of Chaos.

TREELORDS

Mightiest of all the denizens of Ghyran are the ancient tree-folk known as the Sylvaneth. Secretive and hostile to outsiders, the Sylvaneth are ruthless in their defence of the natural world, from the tiniest shrub to the most massive wyrmwood. And greatest among the Sylvaneth are the treelords, noble spirits suffused with potent life-magic and pledged to the Lady Alarielle. Strongstem is a prime example: with his towering size and rootlike strength, he is the master of his forest domain.

BRANCHWYCHES

The wizards of the Sylvaneth are known as branchwyches, magical beings renowned for their skill in combat and battle magic. The branchwych known as Litheroot is young for her kind,

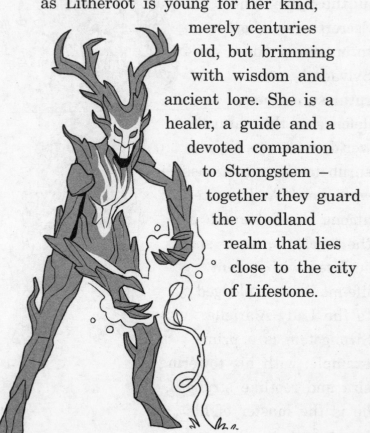

merely centuries old, but brimming with wisdom and ancient lore. She is a healer, a guide and a devoted companion to Strongstem – together they guard the woodland realm that lies close to the city of Lifestone.

ALARIELLE

Also known as the Queen of the
Radiant Wood, the Lady Alarielle is
the protector of Ghyran, and of all
living things throughout the Mortal
Realms. In her soulpod glades she
grew the first Sylvaneth, giving them
guardianship over her beloved land.
But when Ghyran was invaded by rot
and plague Alarielle despaired, hiding
herself away for many centuries. It was
only when Sigmar began his great war
against Chaos that Alarielle was reborn,
and her mighty spirit-song was once
again heard throughout the forests and
valleys of Ghyran.

ASHNAKH

First known to Kiri and
the others as the
Hooded Lady, the
dark power who
has kidnapped
Vertigan is in fact
named Ashnakh, a
mighty sorceress
who resides
in Shyish,
the Realm
of Death.
But that
realm was not her
birthplace – like
her old acquaintance
Vertigan she was actually born in
Lifestone, and her fate is inextricably
bound to that crumbling city. Right now
her purpose is to gather together all
seven birthmarks – to what evil end,
our heroes still do not know.

DEADWALKERS

Undead warriors brought back to life by the foul magic of the sorceress Ashnakh, the deadwalkers are little more than slaves, walking corpses without intelligence or free will. Utilised both as cheap labour in Ashnakh's warpstone mine and as fodder for her army, the deadwalkers are utterly expendable. But that doesn't mean they're not dangerous: overwhelming their enemy by sheer force of numbers, the deadwalkers can be a fighting force to be reckoned with.

GRIFFONS

With the body of a lion, the wings of an eagle and terrifying twin heads, the griffon is an ancient and noble creature much feared and revered throughout the realm of Ghyran. Thanks to their sharp claws, fierce beaks and ability to soar over the heads of the enemy, griffons are highly prized as battle-steeds. But these creatures are almost impossible to tame, preferring the isolation of mountain passes and other remote environments.

THANIS

Bearing the mark of
Aqshy, the Realm of Fire,
twelve-year-old Thanis
is tough, hot-tempered
and fiercely loyal
to her friends.
With her flame-red
hair and imposing
stature she can make
newcomers feel nervous,
but deep down Thanis
is a gentle soul: vigilant,
steadfast and determined
to do good in the
world. Growing up an
orphan on the streets
of Lifestone, she was forced to fend
for herself from an early age. But she
found companionship, first with her
best friend, Kaspar, then with Vertigan
and the others at the Arbour, whose
lives she'd do anything to protect.

THE ARBOUR SEED

Inspired by
the mighty
airships of the
Kharadron, a
race of flying
Duardin, the
Arbour Seed was
designed and built
by the young
inventor Alish.
Powered by steam
and strange chemicals,
the *Seed*'s central balloon
or 'envelope' supports a gondola
built from old bookcases and scraps
of wood, able to carry up to seven
passengers. An entirely unique mode
of transport, the *Arbour Seed* has
never actually flown – until now...

KASPAR

The most secretive and
sneaky of Vertigan's
little band,
thirteen-year-old
Kaspar's early
years are shrouded
in mystery. Who his
parents were or what
their fate might
have been no one knows,
but the boy spent his
youth on the streets of
Lifestone, stealing to eat and struggling
to survive. Although he bears the
mark of Shyish, the Realm of Death,
Kaspar tries his best to be good: he's
smart, resourceful and seems devoted
to his companions, particularly his best
friend Thanis, with whom he's endured
many tough times. But he also has
a tendency to keep secrets, some of
which may affect his friends in ways
they can't yet imagine...

ABOUT THE AUTHOR

Tom Huddleston is an author and freelance film journalist based in East London. His first novel, future-medieval fantasy *The Waking World*, was published in 2013. He's since penned three instalments in the official *Star Wars: Adventures in Wild Space* series and is also the writer of the *Warhammer Adventures: Realm Quest* series. Find him online at www.tomhuddleston.co.uk.

ABOUT THE ARTISTS

Magnus Norén is a freelance illustrator and concept artist living in Sweden. His favourite subjects are fantasy and mythology, and when he isn't drawing or painting, he likes to read, watch movies and play computer games with his girlfriend.

Cole Marchetti is an illustrator and concept artist from California. When he isn't sitting in front of the computer, he enjoys hiking and plein air painting. Warhammer Adventures is his first project working with Games Workshop.

An Extract from book four
Flight of the Kharadron
by Tom Huddleston
(out November 2019)

The sky-beast's mighty jaws snapped shut and Alish clung to the railing as the *Arbour Seed* was swallowed, sluicing from side to side as they raced down the creature's throat. All around them she could hear the *thump-thump* of the monster's blood, its huge heart pumping.

The flying creature had come upon them in the skies above the city of Lifestone, as Alish was struggling to pilot the airship home. It had hunted them through the clouds, snapping up

the *Arbour Seed* and its passengers
as they tumbled towards the ground.
Now they were sliding down its gullet,
lost in warm, pounding heat.

Thick liquid splashed over the railing
and Alish felt a wave of disgust as
it clung to her clothes, her skin, her
hair. She wiped herself clean but the
stench was hideous, rotting meat and
bile. They tipped forwards and Elio
cried out, clutching her hand as the
incline grew steeper and they picked
up speed, rocketing along the pink,
fleshy tunnel.

Alish looked around in confusion.
'Wait,' she said, almost to herself.
'How can I see?'

'This stuff's luminous,' Elio said,
wiping a splash of bile from his face.
He was right; it was glowing a faint,
almost ghostly green, lighting up the
pulsating passage.

'It stings, too, if you leave it too
long,' Kiri said, mopping her face with
her sleeve. 'Try not to get any on you.'

Suddenly a shape loomed from the shadows ahead – a razor-sharp beak and massive spread wings. But the bird was dead, Alish saw, black feathers clinging to rotted bones. It must've been swallowed just like them, and become lodged in the creature's throat. The passage tilted downwards and the airship picked up speed, the wave of bile carrying them past strange openings in the walls of the gullet, like corridors leading deeper into the creature's gut.

'It must have multiple stomachs,' Elio said in wonder. 'I've heard of this, some creatures have these – aaaagh!'

The passage suddenly opened out, and for a moment they were falling, saliva raining around them. There was a giant splash as they landed, dropping into a pool of wet, sticky, faintly glowing warmth. Alish took a breath, trying to calm herself. They were still alive, and that was a good start.

The glow lit up the sides of the gondola, the wrecked balloon overhead and their five damp, startled faces.

'Look on the bright side,' Kaspar said. 'At least we're not going to crash any more.'

Thanis snorted, then shook her head. 'This isn't funny. I don't know what it is yet, but it's definitely not funny.'

'Wait, is there... is there someone over there?' Kiri whispered, pointing.

Alish peered out. In the queasy green light she could see the walls of the chamber, pink and fleshy and veined in blue. There were shapes in the gloom; white bones and furred remains, and the black shell of some vast flying insect. And following Kiri's finger she could indeed see figures in the dark, pale and motionless, staring at them from empty, eyeless sockets.

'Looks like they've been here a while,' Elio whispered. 'What's that contraption they're sitting in?'

It was shaped roughly like their

own airship, but slightly larger and constructed from steel instead of wood. The skeletal figures slumped inside, armoured in bronze and leather, wispy beards still clinging to their masked faces.

'They're Kharadron!' Alish realised. 'The Duardin who worked out how to fly. They must have been swallowed too, like we were.'

There was a sudden flash of light and Alish felt the strangest sensation, a sort of tugging in her muscles as though she'd suddenly moved without moving.

'What was that?' Thanis whispered. 'I feel... like I've felt it before.'

'You have,' Kiri said. 'It felt like it did when we went through the gnawhole into the Skaven tunnels. And like it did when I came through the Realmgate.'

'You mean we're in a different realm?' Kaspar asked. 'How is that possible?'

Elio's eyes lit up. 'I've read about this. There are supposed to be creatures, very rare ones, that can actually move between realms of their own accord. It's like how some fish can travel from the salt sea to fresh water, to lay their eggs. They feed in one realm, and spawn in another.'

Kiri frowned. 'Maybe we'll get lucky and it'll take us to Shyish, so we can find Vertigan.'

Their master had been stolen by a sorceress named Ashnakh, and they still weren't sure why. It had something to do with the birthmarks each of them bore. They'd been on their way back to the besieged city of Lifestone to look for clues when the sky-beast had eaten them.

'Do you have any idea how big each realm is?' Elio asked. 'Even if we happened to end up in Shyish, the chances of us finding where she's keeping him are—'

'Um, this is all very fascinating,'

Thanis said, peering over the side. 'But we've got a bigger problem. Alish, look!'

Alish joined her, looking down. They were floating in a lake of bile with foul bubbles erupting from it, emitting clouds of stinking gas. But there was a darker mist in the air too, hissing from the side of the airship.

'It's dissolving the wood,' she said, fighting to keep the panic from her voice. 'It's like Kiri said, it burns like acid. It's eating the airship!'

Elio wrung his hands. 'Is there anything you can do?'

Alish gulped. 'I didn't really plan for this. I thought we might hit something or fall out of the sky, I didn't think we'd get swallowed by some giant big massive—'

'Hey,' Kiri said. 'Take a breath, and let's figure out what to do.'

'Well there's only one way out of here,' Thanis said, looking up. The creature's gullet was a pulsating portal overhead, saliva dripping from it.

'Technically there's two,' Kaspar pointed out. 'But I don't really want to try the other route, do you?'

He's trying to seem calm, Alish thought, *but deep down he must be as scared as any of us*. Kaspar's hand had slipped inside his shirt and he was touching something restlessly, his fingers wrapped around it. Alish frowned – a few days before, he had come into possession of a pendant, a black pyramid that turned out to have come from the same sorceress that had stolen Vertigan. He said he'd thrown it away, but could he have lied to them?

'Look, the Duardin ship hasn't dissolved,' Kiri was saying. 'The stuff must eat through wood but not steel. If we can get there, it'd at least buy us some time.'

Alish nodded, pulling a screw-loosener from her tool belt,

wishing her hands would stop shaking. 'If we detach one of the struts that hold up the boiler pipe we could use it to push ourselves along,' she said. 'The stern-side strut's the longest, if we take out the bolts here and here we should be able to... what's that?'

They froze, listening. The sound seemed to come from all around them, a distant buzzing.

'Listen,' Elio said. 'The heart. I think it's speeding up.'

He was right – the creature's pulse had quickened, pounding through the fleshy walls. The air seemed to grow more stifling, the bubbles in the bile fizzing more rapidly.

'Is it...' Elio asked, confused. 'Is it scared?'

Kiri grinned. 'Maybe something's after it. That'll teach it to go around eating people.'

'But you have to wonder,' Kaspar said. 'What could possibly scare something this big?'

The buzzing grew louder, seeming to circle around them. The beast's heartbeat thudded faster. Then suddenly the entire chamber started to revolve around them, bile splashing over the railings as the creature rolled. Alish leapt back, avoiding a surge of stinging green slime as the *Arbour Seed* tipped then crashed back down, riding the steepening wave. The walls were closing in, the stomach contracting. There was a deep, guttural roar, the creature bellowing. But it was suddenly cut off, muffled somehow, as though the beast had been gagged, though that was surely impossible.

'What's happening?' Thanis cried out as the lake of bile boiled madly.

Elio grabbed the railing. 'Everybody, hang on!'

A geyser erupted beneath them and the *Arbour Seed* was lifted upwards, the walls of the chamber dropping away as they shot towards the ceiling and through the opening in its centre.

Borne on a green wave they were swept back into the gullet, clinging on desperately. They passed the different openings and the lodged skeleton, driven on by a crashing wall of thick liquid.

Then suddenly they stopped, waves of bile crashing past them like a fast-flowing river. Alish looked up.

'We're stuck!'

Part of the balloon's support structure had become wedged in the creature's throat, pinning them in place. The walls throbbed around them, the monster hacking and coughing desperately.

'Can you cut us loose?' Kiri shouted over the din.

Alish crouched by the strut, feeling for the bolts. They were stiff, but she tugged on her screw-loosener and the first one came free, dropping into her hand. The creature coughed again, breath and saliva whooshing past them – it was like trying to work in a gale.

Then the other bolt dropped out and the strut crashed down, leaving an angry purple mark on the roof of the gullet. The sky-beast gave another cough and the *Arbour Seed* was thrown forwards. Alish saw light up ahead, the creature's teeth like stalactites in the mouth of a cave.

Then they were free, and falling.